Find you.
Happiness &

HOME
IN
Paradise

K Gipsm
O

TEXAS
SUMMER
NIGHTS

HOME
IN
Paradise

KRISTI COPELAND

Twisted Tales Publishing 2022

Home in Paradise

Copyright © 2022 Kristi Copeland

Twisted Tales Publishing 2022

For information contact :

https://kristicopelandwriter.com/

Cover design: Pretty Indie: Book Cover Designs

Editor: Kerri Boehm

Formatting Template : Derek Murphy

ISBN: 978-1-7376339-5-2 (paperback) 978-1-7376339-4-5 (ebook)

For my husband:

My love, my king, my everything.

CONTENTS

Great Pyrenees

Friday, July 3, 2020

DARKNESS COVERED School House Road as it had every morning at 4:00am. Brad Daniels rubbed his eyes and yawned, still trying to wake up. Any other day it didn't matter if he was a few minutes late to the store, but because he had an appointment with his largest customer, Brad didn't want to keep him waiting.

The headlights of Brad's F-250 reflected off a road sign that indicated a curve ahead. Always alert for deer on the country road, Brad startled as a huge fluffy object darted into his path. He swerved into the other lane to avoid the animal, but a loud *thunk* on the passenger-side fender made him cringe. "Damn it, it is too early for this shit."

A large, white dog appeared in the rearview mirror; it seemed to look directly at Brad as it tried to get up, failed, and fell to the road. Memories of Brad's first best friend, a Great Pyrenees, came to mind as he stopped the truck.

From the day the dog had wandered onto the Daniel's property, he and the boy were inseparable. Brad had named the stray Hunter and promised he would always have a home. In exchange, Hunter offered Brad his unconditional friendship. Both of his brothers hated that old dog and told him that it was the only friend he would ever have. Then came the day that still gave Brad nightmares.

"Damn it all to Hell." Pushing the door open and the memory aside, Brad grabbed his pistol from the dash and a shovel from the bed of the truck. Just in case. Because Brad had started his career as a butcher, he didn't have a problem putting a slug into whatever animal needed to be put out of its misery. After taking one look at the dog's matted long hair as he laid crumpled in the middle of the road, Brad holstered his gun.

The dog gazed at Brad with sad, brown eyes for a few seconds as if asking for help before he laid his head on the pavement, whimpering. Brad knew he had to do whatever he could to save him; a bullet just wouldn't do for this guy. "It's ok, fella," Brad whispered, crouching beside the dog. Dirty fur met his hand and, as he stroked the dog's head, blood smeared his palm. "I'm here. I'll help you."

The Animals of Paradise Vet Clinic was a half mile up the road. Because Brad passed by it at least twice every day, he knew the doctor lived in the house adjacent to the office. After Brad secured the dog in the back seat, he dialed the number to his customer. "Carl. Yeah, buddy, I'm sorry. I'm going to be a little late."

∩ ∩ ∩

DRESSED IN A MICHIGAN State T-shirt and black yoga pants, Julia Baker rubbed her eyes as she trudged to the door. Her mass of blonde curls had been pulled into a ponytail. A frown surrounded deep blue eyes. *So...early*, she thought. *What could possibly be so important at this hour?*

Even without makeup, Julia's appearance enticed Brad. He could almost picture lying beside her after a wild night of passion. Her petite frame and captivating eyes left him stunned. He cleared his throat, removed his cowboy hat, and shook the sexy thoughts from his mind. "Doctor Baker? I need your help. I hit a dog just down the road and I think he's hurt pretty bad. He's in my back seat."

Caught off-guard by the strangers deep brown eyes and full lips, Julia pushed the attraction to the back of her mind, "Let's take a look." As she followed the man, she couldn't help but notice how his jeans fit his nicely plump backside and she loved men in cowboy hats. She wondered if the adrenalin stemmed from the emergency or the instant fascination.

The truck had been parked sideways in the driveway and was still running. The man opened a back door to allow Julia access to the injured dog. After a brief glance, she put her hands on the matted fur and searched for wounds. As the dog let out a low growl, she didn't flinch. Instead, she seemingly read his mind. She spoke, almost cooing, to the dog. "Okay, boy. I know it hurts." The dog lifted his head and whimpered making Julia tilt her head and smile. "You're hungry? I have some great kibble and some canned goodies for you in the clinic. No worries, fella." Her voice shifted out of the baby talk she'd used for the dog. "Follow me."

Brad had never met a woman so confident and calm under pressure. She knew exactly what to do and how to express what she needed from him. As he followed her to the clinic, he grinned; the way her yoga pants outlined every curve made his heartrate increase. Impatience took away from the moment—he had a customer waiting.

Julia unlocked the door and turned on the lights. She pointed to an exam room to the left and Brad carried the dog over the threshold.

Once they had the dog on the exam table, Julia asked so many questions Brad could barely keep up, "How fast were you going? Didn't you see him? Why didn't you slow down? Do you know the owner? He'll need X-rays. He's severely malnourished. Must be a drop-off. Damn, I hate people sometimes."

"What?" After Brad assumed Julia was talking about him as one of the people she sometimes hated, his eyebrows formed a V. He decided it was easier to ignore most of the questions and answered what he thought was the most important. "I've seen this guy quite a few times along the road over the past couple weeks, but I didn't think he was a stray. Figured he was just wandering."

A white cat without a tail jumped on the counter beside the exam table and meowed. "Peanut, I'm busy," the doctor crooned while she examined the dog's limbs. "I'll feed you later, baby."

This woman is crazy, talking to cats and interpreting dog whimpers. Anxious to get back on the road, Brad raised his eyebrows, shook his head, and began to pace. He looked at his watch and said, "Look, doc. I have ten head of cattle waiting to be processed. I really need to go."

Cradling the dog's leg in her hand, she paused the exam to confront her impatient client. "What, exactly, do you mean by processed?"

5

"Processed." Brad failed to cover his condescending tone. "The act of butchering animals for human consumption."

Julia's eyebrows knitted together as she continued to glare. She tilted her head and pursed her lips, forcing herself to not speak.

"They're going to be ground beef in a couple of hours. Does that make sense?" Brad added.

Heat rose up her neck and her breathing increased. "If they're just going to die anyway, I hardly think they'll be upset at your tardiness." *Asshole*, Julia added silently.

Frustrated, Brad huffed "Jesus," under his breath. "Just fix him up and I'll stop by later to pay the bill, ok?"

"You honestly think it's that easy?" Julia gently released the dog's leg and turned to face the gorgeous cowboy who had already found an uncanny way of pushing her buttons. She forced the attraction to the side and said, "You just drop him off and get on with your business? This dog is going to need a lot of aftercare. His broken leg will need to be carefully monitored. God only knows what damage has been done internally. What are you going to do with him after I just fix him up? Dump him back on the road? I won't let that happen."

"Maybe I shoulda just put a bullet in his head and put him out of his misery..." Brad interrupted and pursed his lips. He didn't mean what he just said but didn't have the extra time to take it back, apologize, and explain. He glanced at his watch again, then lifted his gaze to Julia and stilled.

Paralyzed with anger, Julia lifted her eyes to meet Brad's stare. "You know what? You need to go. Now. Just get out."

"Gladly." He turned to leave.

Julia followed him to the door. She wasn't finished with him, "Must be nice to be so selfish and not worry about anything besides yourself. Ugh!" Enraged, she slammed the door behind him.

Julia's words stopped him in his tracks; no one had ever called him selfish before.

∩ ∩ ∩

"I'M SO SORRY, LANIE. I have to take care of this dog. He's been here since four o'clock this morning and he's still not stable." Julia explained to her friend, Lanie Green—soon-to-be Walker—over the phone. "Some guy dropped him off and promised he would be back later to pay his bill but never showed. He's not chipped—the dog, not the guy. A nice woman that Teri knows offered to take him as a foster as soon as I give him permission to leave. The dog, not the guy.

Julia chuckled at her own inside joke. "Gave me a

credit card and everything. Guess the loser that hit him won't have to worry about forking out a couple grand for someone else's drop-off." She sighed. "I promise tomorrow will go off without a hitch. I've been in enough weddings and watched enough Lifetime movies to know how to be part of a wedding party. Besides, you'll have Sarah and Pam there to help."

Lanie laughed. "Don't worry, Julia. I absolutely understand. Thanks for letting me know." She hung up the phone and filled in her fiancé, Max Walker, on what happened. "Of course, there's always something that goes wrong when planning a wedding. Who would ever have guessed that a veterinarian would have an emergency the day of the rehearsal dinner?" With a roll of her eyes, Lanie dismissed the slight interruption in her plans.

Max chuckled. "Well, knowing Julia, she'll be at the wedding long enough for the ceremony, go back to care for that dog, then come back for a drink. She has the best heart. How long has it been since she broke up with that pathetic excuse of a man? I really hope she and Brad hit it off tomorrow."

Lanie and Julia had met two years before at the Marker Cellars Winery, just outside of Sunset. Since that day, they had been friends; their mutual experience of moving south from Michigan cemented their bond.

Max and Brad used to play in the same band back in the day and had been supportive friends whenever the other was going through relationship struggles. Their love of music and pretty girls led them to becoming fast friends.

A wedding was the best place for friends of friends to be set up, as Julia always said, and she had been willing to meet Max's friend. After a tumultuous relationship ended three months prior, she was ready to meet a truly nice guy. Lanie promised she wouldn't be disappointed.

Walker Wedding

Saturday, July 4, 2020

STANDING IN FRONT of a full-length mirror, Lanie Green smiled at her reflection, a tall brunette dressed in a white tulle-and-lace wedding gown. With her hair swept into an up-do, she felt both elegant and sexy. The sweetheart neckline, adorned with a heart-shaped diamond necklace, revealed a respectable amount of cleavage. Floral and paisley prints on the outer layer of tulle displayed a rustic vibe that matched the event décor.

"Lanie, you look just divine!" Julia spritzed the bride with rose water as the final step in preparation. "Beautiful, lovely, stunning. You couldn't have chosen a more perfect dress. I guarantee Max's mind will officially be blown." She backed away from Lanie and held her arms open.

"You're so sweet, Julia." Lanie accepted a light

embrace to protect hours of primping. "Thank you for everything you've done to help prepare for the wedding. I'm so excited that this day is finally here."

Chatter from the other bridesmaids reminded Lanie that this day had already been wonderful. Time spent with some of her favorite people allowed her to appreciate the unique relationships she had developed with each of them. She turned to address her bridal party as they stood before her, ready to lead her down the aisle.

Each of the girls had expressed her own style with the dress they'd chosen for the wedding. The only request from Lanie was that it be a shade of lavender. Julia was wearing an elegant chiffon dress with a deep V-neck, flutter sleeves, and a slit that ended mid-thigh, while Sarah's spaghetti straps and full skirt showed off her thin frame. Pam, the most adventurous of the group, rocked a one-shoulder crinkle chiffon with a slit almost to her hip.

"You all look so beautiful. Thank you for being here and celebrating such a special day with me. The photographer took the boys out early to bide us some time, so we'll do our pictures after the ceremony." A sincere smile reached Lanie's lips as she gazed at Julia.

"I'm so sorry, Lanie."

"You've apologized a million times, and it's ok. We

all understand that you had to tend to a patient this morning. We'll do the final pictures later. Not a big deal." Lanie shook her head and raised her eyebrows. "You're paired with Brad, by the way. You know, the guy Max and I have been dying to set you up with. You're just perfect for each other."

Exaggerating her annoyance, Julia sighed, rolled her eyes, and then added a wink. "He better be hot."

"Honestly, Julia, none of us were ready on time either," Sarah reassured her. "We've been busy talking about girl stuff all day."

"And drinking wine from this fantastic venue," Pam added. "What an ingenious idea to have your wedding at a winery. Perfect for all of us wine-o's!"

Lanie whispered something to Julia about the honeymoon. They leaned into each other and giggled. "You're so bad," Julia covered her mouth with her hand before turning serious. "When we met two years ago, would you have ever imagined that this is where your life would be now? I am so incredibly happy for you and honored to be a part of your wedding party."

With a shake of her head, Lanie raised her eyebrows, "Never in my wildest dreams would I think that a Nashville country star would propose to me on stage. I'm still in shock!"

"Dreams really do come true." Sarah smiled and

Pam nodded.

The girls raised their glasses in yet another toast. "To love," they said in unison and then finished their drinks.

∩∩∩

MARKER CELLARS WINERY provided a picturesque area set in the middle of the vineyard exclusively used to perform wedding ceremonies. After the ceremony, guests would follow a path that led to the event center to allow the wedding party extra time to finish with the photographer.

Surprised by his level of anxiety, Max shifted from foot to foot and did his best to keep from wringing his hands as he waited for the groomsmen to escort the bridesmaids down the aisle. Smiles from his granny in the front row helped keep him calm.

Excited whispers reached the guests in the back row as the girls took their place behind a barrier of vines. Unable to completely see the groomsmen, they took their signal from Jared, one of the ushers. Max had introduced him as a friend and bandmate from Nashville.

Julia stood behind Sarah, Lanie's best friend from Michigan and Maid of Honor, who was paired with

Max's best man, his dad. Sarah almost missed her cue because she was so enamored with Jared; she couldn't take her eyes off him. He had to literally touch her to snap her out of her daydream.

As the best man and Maid of Honor walked toward each other, Julia busied herself by making sure her dress was wrinkle-free and her necklace hung straight. White daisies tied in a bundle were adjusted so the bow was perfectly centered.

"Julia."

Startled by Jared's voice, Julia raised her head and took the first steps toward her groomsman. "Oh, my god. No." She shook her head and stopped in her tracks, forcing Pam to bump into her back. "That can't be him."

"Julia? What's wrong?" Pam asked in a loud whisper and touched her arm.

"N-nothing," Julia stammered and glanced behind her, trying to steady her stance. "It's okay. Let's do this," she said before glaring at the man in front of her. As they stepped closer, Julia's suspicion was confirmed. The jerk that dropped the dog at her clinic was standing in front of her, wearing a smile as bright as the sun. *If he wasn't such a jackass, I would be thrilled to walk down the aisle with this handsome man. Wait. What? Stop it, Julia. He's a tool, remember?*

The groomsmen wore black jackets, white button-up shirts, blue jeans, and black cowboy hats. Brad looked so much different than he had the previous day; his smile had changed his entire demeanor. It disturbed Julia that he was laughing at her scowl, but the way he gazed at her gave her chills. Good chills. She almost thought he would grab her and kiss her in front of all the wedding guests. And she might even let him.

Oh, shit. The wedding. She had almost forgotten where she was. She forced a smile, took a deep breath, and another step toward Brad. As she grasped his elbow, she whispered, "How are you here?"

"Hey there, beautiful." Brad chuckled. "I guess you would know if you didn't have an emergency last night during the rehearsal dinner."

Julia turned her head toward Brad, the fake smile replaced by a sneer. "I wasn't here because of you. Speaking of you didn't even bother to come back to pay for your mistake. Typical." Picking up her pace, Julia attempted to force Brad to walk faster. The last thing she wanted was to touch this pitiful human for one more second than she had to.

"What are you talking about?" Brad hissed, slowing the pace despite Julia. "I sent my secretary to your place with my credit card. She told me it was all good."

"Oh, that was *you?* I didn't know." She winced then offered a sincere, "I guess I should thank you."

15

"Didn't you look at the name on the card? Brad Daniels?"

"Yes, but I thought it was her husband's card. You didn't tell me your name. I was angry and you didn't bother to leave any information before you left."

"Before you kicked me out."

"Yeah." Julia smirked and tilted her head, pleased with herself for forcing him out of her office the previous day. "Whatever."

Brad's smile turned to a frown before he whispered, "How is he?"

The simple yet compassionate question touched Julia's heart and her shoulders relaxed. She flashed a slight, genuine grin. "He'll be okay."

∩∩∩

THOMAS RHETT'S "BLESSED" played as the DJ introduced the bride and groom at the beginning of their first dance as a married couple. Guests stopped what they were doing and turned their attention to the newlyweds. The couple embraced, smiled, and laughed as the song lyrics described how each of them felt; far more than lucky. Max spun Lanie as he sang to her, adoration radiating from his eyes.

The bridal party joined as couples at the edge of the

dance floor. Although Julia found Brad extremely sexy, she couldn't get over the fact he made his living as a butcher. She had been anxiously awaiting this moment all day, dancing with a man who slaughtered animals. She tried not to shudder at the visual. *How could Lanie think we would possibly be a match when my personal and professional goal is to save animals' lives?*

Chris Stapleton's raspy voice as he sang "More of You" accompanied the balance of the wedding party for their time in the spotlight. Brad pulled Julia a little too close for her liking so he could whisper in her ear. "Have I told you that you look radiant in that dress, Julia? Just beautiful."

Peppermint mixed with a woody citrus fragrance reached Julia's senses. She pictured the men drinking shots of Schnapps in the parking lot, like most everyone did at wedding receptions. The scent of her favorite Giorgio Armani cologne, Acqua di Gio, made her dizzy; she was forced to grasp Brad tighter to keep her balance.

Even though Julia enjoyed the compliment, she pushed back and rolled her eyes. "Why are you being so nice to me?" She was positive that her cheeks had turned pink from the wine, not the attraction to the man whose hand rested on the small of her back.

"Why wouldn't I be nice to you?" The brim of his cowboy hat brushed the top of Julia's hair as he leaned close again. "You seem like a good person that I might want to be friends with. Can't you just take the compliment? Besides..." His smiled faded as he captured her gaze, his brown eyes turned black. "That color of lavender brings out a sparkle in your eye." He brushed a strand of hair away from her face.

A small gasp escaped her lips as she attempted to ignore the intimate gesture and struggled to not let his touch affect her. "You're so full of shit," she whispered, her eyes wide.

Brad steadied his hold on her, threw his head back, and let out a genuine laugh.

�∩∩∩

"THINK SHE'LL END UP with Jared tonight?" Julia nodded toward Sarah and nudged Pam. Music drifted from the speakers, inspiring guests to move their feet in an alcohol-induced rhythm across the dance floor. The Maid of Honor danced to Billy Idol's "Mony Mony" and shook her body suggestively as Jared attempted, and failed, to keep his hands to himself.

"She needs to wipe that drool off her chin first," Pam responded with a laugh. "That girl couldn't be less obvious if she tried." With a tilt of her head, she added, "I used to look at Jason with those same hungry eyes.

We were so hot for each other when we first started dating..." Her words trailed off when she spotted her husband across the room.

"And now?" Julia asked, curious about life after marriage.

"Oh, nothing's changed," Pam turned to her new friend and winked. "He's in for a treat tonight; weddings bring back memories of our dating days."

"Good for you. I can only dream of finding a man like that."

"What about Brad? Lanie said she's been dying to set you up with him. I've seen how he looks at you, but you've been sneering at him all day."

"What do you mean?" Julia frowned.

"Come on, girl. It's written all over your face. What's the story with you two?" Pam rested her chin in her hand, waiting for a response.

Groomsmen gathered in front of the DJ stand. Their black cowboy hats hid specific identities, but Julia could pick out Brad by the shape of his backside. As if he could feel her stare, he turned and caught her eye. He tipped the front of his hat just enough to let her know he had his eye on her too.

Unsure if it was the heat of the day or the glances from Brad that made her temperature rise, Julia took a deep breath to calm her speeding heartbeat. "Even if he is gorgeous and that cowboy hat is the biggest turn on, he's an ass." Returning her attention to Sarah, she continued. "For one, he hit a dog and dumped him at my clinic at four in the morning. He was in such a hurry to leave that he didn't wait to find out if the dog would be ok, or even leave his name and number so I could contact him."

"But he didn't leave the dog alongside the road to die, right?" Pam raised her eyebrows.

"Well...no. But..." Julia sighed. "He kills animals for a living. How could anyone do that?"

"Oh." Pouring wine into both of their glasses, Pam handed one to Julia and sat back in her chair. "Wait, what do you mean by that? Like he runs around town killing dogs, cats, rabbits, and gerbils for money?"

Julia laughed at the absurdity of the question. "No. He's a butcher."

"So, he makes it possible for people to feed their families and enjoy healthy economical meals instead of surviving on rice and beans?"

Julia's brow furrowed as she focused on the liquid in her glass and thought about Pam's question. She almost felt a little guilty for treating him like he did something wrong.

"That's horrible." Pam hid her smirk with a drink of Moscato.

HOME IN PARADISE

Charlie

Monday, July 6, 2020

SURROUNDED BY STAINLESS steel, Brad and his older brother, Greg, worked without words. As usual, the radio played country music in the background while the men cleaned and cut the meat. Lulled by music and repetition, Brad remembered his first dog, Hunter.

Baths were the one thing Hunter despised, but Brad's dad told him that if he wanted to keep that mangy dog, he had to give him a bath every week. Each time Hunter got wet, he then rolled in the nearest grass-free patch of dirt, just like a horse. After enough baths, Brad figured out a way to keep the dog clean during his roll by spreading an old blanket out beside the wash area. It worked twice.

On that last day, Brad called for his dog all morning. Hunter was never far away and when he didn't come running, Brad's stomach sank. He started his search in the barn and found Hunter laying in one of the open stalls. His white fur had been stained red around his head and shoulder. At the sound of his name, the dog tried to raise his head but could only whimper. A twitch of the dog's tail sent Brad running for his dad.

"We've got five more sides hanging in the cooler that have to be finished today. Want me to call Pop back to come help?" Greg asked without taking his eyes off the project in front of him. When Brad didn't answer, he glanced up to find his brother daydreaming as he worked. "Brad!"

"Yeah?"

Greg smiled and repeated the question.

"That's not a bad idea; we could use a break. If Pop helps, we could knock the rest of this out in no time. Sherri can handle the front counter." To prepare for the next piece of beef, Brad wiped down and sanitized his station. It wasn't like him to agree to one of Greg's ideas so quickly.

"What's on your mind, bro?"

"I hit a dog Friday morning." Brad winced and shook his head. "Looked just like Hunter."

"I know. Sherri heard about it and offered to foster him."

"What?" Knives rattled against the stainless steel as Brad set them down, his hand unsteady. He needed to know more. "Sherri has him? Where?"

With a nod toward the door, Greg led his brother to his wife and the company secretary, Sherri's, office. Inside an extra-large dog crate, the Great Pyrenees that Brad had delivered to The Animals of Paradise Vet Clinic a few days before wagged his tail at the sound of voices. He tried to sit up before he settled on his side. The cast on his back leg and bandages around his midsection made it difficult to move.

"She wants to keep an eye on him and knows you're a softie when it comes to dogs. Didn't think you'd mind."

"No, it's fine." Brad shook his head before he crouched beside the crate.

"Guess I'll go call Dad," Greg said to himself and walked away.

"Are you ok, pal?" The cold metal panel of the crate felt like a prison cell to Brad, but he understood the need for protection. "I'm so sorry I hit you. I swerved the second I saw you I swear." Brad moved to the front of the crate, sat on the floor, and opened the door enough to put his hand inside. Fur from the dog's hip filled his hand as he touched a spot that didn't look injured. "Doc fixed you up good, huh? She told me you're going to make it. I'm so glad you're ok."

The dog wagged his tail and moved his eyes toward Brad as if accepting his apology. "I know you're in pain, so I'll leave you alone and let you rest, but I'll come back to check on you, ok?"

Voices outside the door proceeded Sherri into her office. "Hey, boss. I see you discovered my little secret. Hope you don't mind that I want to keep this guy close." A knowing smile spread across her face. "Sounds like y'all had some catching up to do. I'm so thankful you're a dog lover. I knew you wouldn't have a problem with me bringing him here to be nurtured back to health. Besides, he reminds you of Hunter."

Brad's eyebrows knitted together in surprise. His sister-in-law seemed to have read his mind.

"I can see it when you look at him. He already loves you for taking him to get help; he appreciates you. Greg warned me that it might be a soft spot, but I think you both need this."

"How long before he's ready to be adopted? Did Doc Baker give you a timeframe?" With his eyes fixed on the dog, Brad moved to the doorway. "I'd like to keep him."

"I knew it!" Sherri grinned and clapped without making too much noise. "I'm not sure, but we'll figure that out. Posters have already been hung all around town, looking for the owner. I heard about this guy from my friend, Teri, Doc Baker's vet tech. She has been bugging me to foster dogs for months. She mentioned his breed and I knew he needed you. Let's hope no one claims him."

Brad nodded and offered a sad smile. "You know me too well, sis."

"Poor thing has been on his own for way too long. Julia said he needs some TLC. Between all the dog lovers at this place, I'm sure he will get plenty of that here." Changing the subject, Sherri asked, "Well, you'll need to choose a name for him" She was surprised by Brad's immediate reply.

"Charlie." Brad smiled when the dog wagged his tail and lifted his head. "His name's Charlie."

"Why Charlie?"

"Look at his reaction. That's his name."

ΩΩΩ

BELLS RANG ABOVE THE door as another customer entered the Paradise Country Market. Murmurs from the store reached Brad's office and he knew his dad would take care of the customer as he had every day for the past year. The store would be closing within ten minutes so it shouldn't be long before the bells rang, again, as the customer left.

"Son, you have a visitor."

A pretty blonde dressed in scrubs stood in the

doorway of Brad's office. He stood to welcome his guest. "Julia. What a nice surprise. What can I do for you?"

"I heard from a little birdie that you're interested in adopting the Great Pyrenees that you brought to me." Julia's smile intoxicated Brad and forced him to mirror her reaction.

"Word sure moves fast in this town." Brad stood and closed the distance between himself and Julia. It was as if he couldn't stand to be more than two feet from her. "Charlie."

"You named him already?" She tilted her head and grinned. Julia's surprise drew a laugh from Brad. "He kind of named himself." Julia shook her head, prompting Brad to explain. "It's the first name that came to me when I picked him up out of the road. Almost like he introduced himself. I know it's weird. Just a feeling, but he seems to like it."

"That's great. I'm so pleased you found each other." She reached out and touched Brad's arm. "I came here to thank you." She glanced at her feet, then found Brad's eyes again. "And apologize."

Brad squinted. "Apologize for what?"

Julia exhaled her deep breath slowly; it was hard for her to admit when she had been wrong, but she felt like it was the right thing to do. "I was quite an ass when you knocked on my door. I'm sure I overreacted and I'm sorry."

"No need to be sorry. It was four in the morning." A step closer and Brad could smell Julia's jasmine-scented perfume. Alarmed by his impatience, Brad tried to stay cool and collected. "Listen, I'd like to take you to lunch. What are you doing, tomorrow?"

Backing through the threshold, Julia shook her head. "Oh, I don't think that's a good idea. I just wanted to thank you, that's all." She turned and made her way through the store aisles and out the front door.

"Julia." Brad's voice reached her ears as she climbed in her car and turned the key.

∩∩∩

SUN SHONE THROUGH the windshield on the short drive back to the clinic. Julia disregarded the warmth on her face; she couldn't break away from the thoughts of previous relationships that she failed to make work. Based on the bad example her parents had set, she was convinced that she attracted a certain type of man on purpose. Either she found the exact replica of her father, or the exact opposite. *Why can't I just find someone normal?*

The mental and physical abuse had been

comfortable and familiar in some sick way. Her boyfriend in high school treated her just as her dad had treated her mom—like she didn't have a voice. When she realized the pattern, she chose a man that was the exact opposite. Her last boyfriend belittled her because she had a successful career and business; he thought she needed to be a stay-at-home wife. Since he spent most evenings in the company of other women, Julia guessed it would be easier for him to cheat if she depended on his support.

Whatever the reason, Julia had been determined to change the type of man she attracted. So far, that meant that there wasn't a man within one hundred miles that fit a different mold, at least not that she had the pleasure of encountering. She had just about given up on finding a good man. Or had she?

The Finish Line

Wednesday, July 8, 2020

AS JULIA STRAIGHTENED cans of cat food on a
shelf in the clinic waiting room, she cradled the phone
on her shoulder, so she could talk to Lanie. "So, about
Brad—"

Lanie didn't let her friend finish the question.
"Look, I know y'all had a rocky start with the dog and
all, but I promise, he's a great guy. Max and I have been
dying for you to meet and get to know each other; we
just know you'll hit it off. He has the best heart, loves his
family, adores animals and music. He's so adventurous
and loves to travel. Just give him a chance, please. I
know you'll be pleasantly surprised."

"I went to see him at the store—" Before she could
finish, Lanie interrupted, again and brought a smile to
Julia's lips.

"You did?" Surprised, Lanie's voice raised two

octaves. "That's great. How did it go?"

"I just wanted to thank him for offering to adopt a dog in need of a forever home. He tried to ask me to lunch, but I couldn't stand being in that place, so I left."

"Opening that store saved his family farm, Julia. He *is* successful..."

"Yeah, about that," Julia said. "Did you really think I would be attracted to someone who kills animals for a living?"

"Julia." After a pause, Lanie put on her persuasive voice. "I know you're thinking about how it goes against everything you stand for, but maybe, just maybe if you look at it in an economical way, in a 'I have to feed my family' kind of way, it does make sense. Local town folks need somewhere to go to have their meat processed. If Brad's family store didn't exist, much of the town wouldn't be able to afford healthy fresh food." Lanie sighed at the silence. "Please don't take this the wrong way, but you of all people should be able to appreciate that. Someone has to do it, right?"

Memories of Julia's childhood flooded back. Her mom would take all five kids with her to the grocery store and more times than she cared to remember, there wasn't enough money to pay for all the food in their cart. Even at such a young age, she understood how embarrassed her mother had been when she chose, in front of other customers in line, which items to put back.

One day, a very kind gentleman behind them offered to pay for their entire cart. Julia's mom tried to refuse the man, but he insisted, even took her through the store to pick out more essentials. That night they ate like kings. Fresh salad joined the wild turkey which had been shot by her father the previous day. They even had dessert.

In central Michigan it was common to hunt and Julia's dad spent more time in the woods than at home. At the end of the day, he would field dress whatever animal was in season; deer, wild turkey, rabbit, duck, whatever fish he could catch, and sometimes, when money had been extra scarce, he would bring home a squirrel or two.

As jubilant as he was to have free food, he was also suspicious that his wife had accepted the handout, as he called it. Julia witnessed her dad grab her mom by the wrist hard enough to leave a bruise. That first time stuck in her brain like a bad replay of long-ago events.

Processing animals wasn't her father's strong suit and more often than she cared to remember, Julia chipped a tooth on bones or buckshot. That last time, a second tooth had been chipped when her dad unexpectedly slapped her for complaining about the food. From then on, she had basically become a vegetarian and refused to touch anything that her dad dressed. A couple weeks later, her dad gave up; he told her that if she wanted to starve herself to death, that was her choice.

Once Julia settled in at Michigan State University and some new friends took her to restaurants that served good cuts of meat, things changed. Not only was she grateful for a nice meal but developed a love for all different kinds of meat.

Julia appreciated that animals needed to be hunted for population control and that people needed to harvest their hunt for economic and health reasons, but why did the one person that made her heart flutter have to be a butcher? She never refused a good cut of meat; filet mignon being her favorite, but that was different. *Right*?

"You're right, Lanie. I do."

∩∩∩

BELLS JINGLED AS THE front door of the Animals of Paradise Pet Clinic opened. Julia wiped her hands on her lab coat and listened as Teri Bridgewater, the best vet tech in the state of Texas, greeted the client. A low, familiar voice asked for her.

Surely, he can't be here? Julia tilted her head to better hear the voices. She questioned her own ears as they grew hot.

"Please have a seat, sir. I will let the doctor know you're here."

Teri rushed through the sliding door to the back room. "Oh, Julia," she sang. "There is a gorgeous man in the waiting room asking for you, but he doesn't have a pet with him." She lifted one eyebrow and grinned. "Want me to find out exactly what Mr. Brad Daniels needs?"

That grin was Teri's telltale sign for 'I can find out anything about anyone with my charming personality.' And she could; she had a knack for asking the perfect questions to put people at ease and made them want to spill the most intimate secrets about their life.

"Oh, my god. You're relentless." With a shake of her head, Julia dismissed the offer. "I'll come out."

Bags of dog food lined one wall and Brad crouched in front of them as he compared the ingredients of two brands. When he heard the chair squeak as Teri returned to the front desk, he stood and turned. He lost his breath when Julia breezed through the door into the waiting room. Her long, blonde curls and radiant smile awakened something in him that he thought was long dead.

"Lunch?" Only able to form one word, Brad smiled. A little giddy, he held out his hand toward the doctor and raised his eyebrows.

The single word gave Julia chills and she could barely blink. *He. Is. Exceptional.* "I...um..." Stammering, she glanced at her watch, not usually this shaken by anything. The time didn't register, so she looked again.

"Your, uh, Teri said your next appointment isn't until two o'clock." He lifted his chin and said, "Come on."

∩∩∩

THE FINISH LINE CAFÉ served the best burgers around, along with various sandwiches and Tex-Mex platters. Lanie had told Julia that most restaurants within fifty miles of Paradise bought their meat from Brad's store. The couple sat at a corner table and waited for the waitress.

"How's Charlie getting along?" Of course, the dog was first and foremost on Julia's mind. She thought discussing him would also be an easy way to break the ice.

"He's doing just fine. Not too happy to be in such a small crate, but Sherri is getting a bigger one today. Probably as we speak."

"I can't tell you how happy it makes me that you're interested in keeping him. Would it be ok if I came to see him sometime?" Julia hoped the request wasn't too forward, but she was accustomed to keeping in touch with her patients for follow-ups and aftercare.

"Of course. Anytime. Just drop by. I'll let everyone know who you are." Even though the tables had been strategically placed throughout the restaurant, during the lunch rush it got crowded, making it difficult to concentrate. "So, you've been in Paradise for how long?" An untouched menu lay on the table between Brad's forearms.

"I moved here a few years ago." Julia turned the menu over, nodded, then moved it to the side. "Needed to get out of the cold Michigan weather. I knew there was a better life waiting for me somewhere warmer." Following Brad's lead, she leaned forward and rested her forearms on the table. "You've been here your entire life, from what Lanie has told me. You must know everything about everyone in this small town."

"Yeah, I do. Almost everyone," leaning back in his chair, Brad didn't take his eyes off Julia. "Sometimes that's not such a good thing."

"I can only imagine. Some of the things that my clients tell me, God, I feel like a bartender," Julia chuckled.

"But I don't know much about you. How is that?" Brad wondered out loud.

"I spend a lot of time in the clinic. I've only recently hired Teri; she's a lifesaver. Finally, after an entire year of running the place on my own, I can actually leave for lunch." A smile formed on Julia's lips and she said, "Thank you for this. Really. It's great to get out."

"You know, when I first saw you at your clinic, I thought you looked familiar; I'm sure we've seen each other in passing. Maybe at the Dollar General or something." Brad's eyes locked with Julia's long enough for her to picture him leaning in for a kiss. "I can't put my finger on it."

Julia looked away and thought *I hope he didn't see me blush. Get a grip, girl.* She unwrapped a straw, stuck it in the water glass, and took a sip to quench her sudden thirst.

A bubbly teenager wearing a striped referee shirt approached the table and took their order with enthusiasm. "Oh, that is our best burger; you'll just love it," she said to Brad after he ordered his usual. He nodded and tried to hide a smirk.

After the waitress walked away, Brad admitted, "I come here at least three times a week and order the exact same thing. From the same girl. She reminds me a little of Luann from King of the Hill." Brad's eyes widened and Julia giggled. He sighed and shook his head. "She's right, though. I do love it."

"So, your family works for you at the store? That was your dad that greeted me yesterday, right?"

"It was. He helps out most days; he still works the farm early in the morning. My brother Greg works with me and his wife, Sherri is our office manager, which is how Charlie ended up at the store. It's pretty much a family affair." Pleased that she didn't appear to be upset with him, anymore, Brad leaned forward and searched Julia's attentive expression. He was dying to know more about the one person in town no one talked about. "Tell me more about you. What made you want to be a vet?"

Smiling to herself, Julia remembered her first dog. "Remington was a German Shepard mix. My brothers and sisters wanted a little ankle biter, but my dad and I agreed on a larger breed. We rescued him from the pound at the last minute; he was next in line to be put down. At least that's how my dad tells the story." A wave of her hand dismissed the doubt.

"Remy and I did everything together. He was my best friend. He was hit by a car when I was fourteen," pursed lips told Brad that the memory was as fresh as if the incident happened yesterday. "My dad refused to take him to the vet. The hunter in him thought it was better to finish the job himself." Julia's eyes began to water. "I cried myself to sleep for weeks. Heard the gunshot in the distance every night."

After she regained her composure, she apologized and continued. "I always thought he could have been saved. If I had just been older and trained, maybe I could have saved him. Like I saved Charlie." Her soft smile touched Brad and he sensed the connection strengthen.

"So, as they say, the rest is history." Memories of high school, college, and everything in between could be shared another day if she decided to see Brad again. At this point, the whole story would surely scare him away, as she learned all too early in life. *Too soon.* "I made it my life goal to save as many of God's creatures as I possibly could. Except snakes." The shudder and a crinkle in Julia's nose brought a chuckle from across the table.

"Unfortunately, I can relate." Brad glanced around the restaurant to make sure his family wasn't in the room and lowered his voice, just in case. "Hunter was a stray Great Pyrenees who came to me when I was nine. We were best friends too. My brothers hated him probably because I had more in common with that old dog than I did with the humans in my family." He lowered his eyes to examine his interlaced fingers. "He died when I was twelve." The rest of the story was better left for a later date. It would not be easy to hide his emotions in a busy restaurant.

ᑎᑎᑎ

"THANKS, AGAIN, FOR lunch, Brad. I needed to get out of the clinic." Julia took a deep breath. The feel of his name on her lips proceeded a warm tingling sensation in her stomach. "Listen, I want to apologize again for the way I acted when we met. I wish we could have been friends before that day. It was nice to talk with you as a person and not as..." Unable to find the right word, Julia paused and glanced out the window of the Jeep.

"Not as the angry, impatient, jerk who dumped a dog on you at four o'clock in the morning?" As Brad pulled into the driveway of the clinic, he turned to Julia with raised eyebrows.

"Mr. Daniels, you read my mind." Julia leaned her head back and let an honest laugh escape.

"Wait here."

As instructed, Julia sat still in the passenger seat as Brad walked around the vehicle and opened her door. She grasped his outstretched hand and slid to the ground, trying, unsuccessfully, not to grin.

Still holding Julia's hand, Brad pulled her into a warm embrace. Her hair, soft on his cheek, smelled of flowers and he wrapped an arm around her thin frame as he had during the wedding party dance the previous weekend. He tried to control his breathing as she wrapped her arms around his neck, but he found himself growing impatient. He wanted nothing more than to kiss her right here. Right now.

Instead, Julia's smooth lips touched Brad's cheek before she pulled away. "Thanks again. I have to go. I'm sure Teri has been bombarded without me here."

She turned toward the clinic door, but Brad refused to release her hand. "Julia?"

With wide eyes, she turned back and held her breath, unable to speak. The undeniable attraction overwhelmed her.

"I have to see you again. Let me take you on a real date—not just lunch, but an adventure." He didn't wait for her to answer. "Friday is my slow day; everything is wrapping up for the week and I usually finish up around three. Can you break away early?"

Hesitant, Julia was not sure she wanted to start something she couldn't finish. *I would love to have a day of fun with a friend, a hot man friend, but can I really fall in love with someone in his line of work? Do I want to put either of us in that position?* "Um. Brad, I'm not sure..."

A twinkle in his eyes let her know he enjoyed a challenge. "Come on, give it a shot. Just say yes. What's the worst that could happen? We become friends and enjoy the day?"

Julia smiled, looked at the ground, and shook her head before meeting his gaze. "Fine. I'll stop all appointments at two-thirty."

Smiling ear to ear, Brad nodded and said, "I'll pick you up at three-fifteen."

Jeep Addiction

Friday, July 10, 2020

"JULIA, YOUR TWO-FIFTEEN is here," Teri announced from behind the reception desk.

Must be Lanie, Julia thought and looked at her watch as she walked into the waiting room. Peanut rested in her normal spot on the counter and Julia ran her hand down the clinic's resident cats back as she did every time she passed.

"Hey, you. Right on time, as always," Julia smiled at Lanie and bent at the waist to greet her next patient. "Sam, how are ya, boy? You ready for your check up?" She scratched the dog behind his ears. He wagged his tail and leaned his weight against her legs in response.

Teri had finished her work for the day and waved as she walked out the door. "Have a good weekend, y'all."

"See you Monday. Thanks, Teri."

"So," Julia led Lanie into the exam room. "How's

married life? Are you pregnant yet?" She giggled.

Lanie laughed and dismissed the suggestion with an eye roll. "It's fantastic! I could have never dreamed of being so happy, so in love, so accepted by another person's family. I feel like we've been together our entire lives. You just wait until someone fits flawlessly into your idea of a perfect man. I swear it's magical."

After Julia finished with Sam's yearly exam and determined that all was well, she introduced her friend to a couple of her patients in need of extended care. "Willy had hip surgery yesterday." She paused at a cage that housed a long-haired black cat with big green eyes.

Lanie gasped. "Hip surgery? What happened to poor Willy?"

"Not exactly sure. He must have been shut in a door or had something hit him hard on his hip; it crushed the femoral head, so I had to remove the broken pieces."

"As if that's just an everyday occurrence." Lanie chuckled and poked a finger into Willy's cage. She cooed at the cat as he rubbed his cheek against her and purred.

Moving to the next cage, Julia said, "Hi there, Scotty," to a white-and-black cat with bandages around his midsection. "This guy here is on life number nine. He escaped the jaws of a coyote. I had to remove a portion of his spleen and sew up four puncture wounds today."

"Oh, my god!" Lanie stood next to the cage and peered at the feline that lay on his side. He lifted his head and squeaked. "Awe, hi there, Scotty." To her friend she said, "You amaze me. How are you so nonchalant about these kinds of surgeries? It sounds so complicated."

Julia shrugged. "Eh, all in a day's work."

"By the way, I'm thrilled you accepted Brad's invitation for today." Lanie smiled. "Remember we're all meeting at the winery tomorrow as a send-off to the rest of the wedding party. Six o'clock. Maybe that could be your second date with Brad. Eh?" She waggled her eyebrows and nudged Julia with her elbow. "Where is he taking you?"

Julia shook her head. "I don't know. He said to dress casual—Jeans and T-shirt casual. I'm intrigued because he's obviously not trying to impress me by throwing money around like some other guys I've dated."

"Yeah, like ol' what's-his-name? Where did he take you for your first date again?"

"Ugh." Julia rolled her eyes and laughed. "Fredrick. The lawyer from Decatur. Thought he was big shit because he represented a sleazy oil tycoon. He took me to an Italian place that one of his buddy's recommended; said they had the best homemade red sauce around."

The memory of their first date still made Julia laugh. "He helped me out of his Lexus and held the door of the restaurant open. I knew from the second we pulled up that it was a dive. It took Fredrick ten seconds after stepping into the place to notice that no one was dressed up, red-and-white plaid plastic tablecloths covered the tables, and"—Julia stifled a giggle—"they had plastic chairs."

Laughter filled the air as the friends reminisced. "Oh, if you could have seen the look on his face. His emotions went from surprise to disgust to anger in a second flat." With a slap to her thigh, Julia laughed so hard that tears ran down her cheeks. "He said 'That fucking James. He's dead,' before pushing me out the door."

∩∩∩

FIFTEEN MINUTES AFTER Lanie drove away, Brad pulled his Jeep into the clinic driveway, put it in park, and pulled the visor down to check his reflection. After a sigh and a smile, he said to himself, "Ok, genius, don't mess this up."

He stepped down from the lifted Jeep and before he reached the door, a petite vision with blonde curls met him on the sidewalk. A catch in his breath surprised him and he had to force himself to exhale. "You look gorgeous," was all he could muster.

Dressed in jeans and an old Michigan State T-shirt, Julia didn't feel gorgeous, but she did feel comfortable. Little did he know, Julia fretted for over an hour trying to decide what to wear. A first date was the time to make an honest impression but because they had already spent time together, it wasn't like they were just meeting. Besides, with Julia, what you saw was what you got; no sense in being deceitful.

She laughed. "Hardly, but thank you. You said casual, so here I am." She stretched her arms out to her side and tilted her head.

Brad's smile widened and he took another step toward Julia. Making the most of her arms still being open, he went in for a hug. As his arms went around her waist, hers naturally settled over his shoulders. Holding her close for a few seconds too long, Brad looked down and tried to hide his smirk as he backed away. "Ready to have some Jeep fun?" he asked when his eyes met hers again. He opened the door and held out his hand for support.

"Some what fun?" Julia grasped his hand and put her foot on the sidestep.

"Jeep fun." He closed her door, walked around to the driver side, and climbed into his seat. "It's kind of a thing. See, everyone who buys a Jeep is automatically welcomed into the Jeep family. There are all kinds of different clubs you can join." Pausing, he glanced at Julia and chuckled at her crinkled forehead and open mouth.

"A club?"

"Yeah. It's a good way to meet people with the same interests and learn the ropes of off-roading." On the twenty-minute drive north, Brad explained that he had always loved off-road machines, like four-wheelers and dirt bikes. Owning a vehicle that can be used for climbing the foothills, mudding, and driving to work all in one—like the Jeep—was right up his alley. He loved to be outdoors and try new things, so buying the Jeep was one of his latest ventures.

They arrived at the Northwest OHV Park gate house on the north side of Bridgeport, stopped to pay the entrance fee, and pulled into a parking spot to look at a map. Brad had been to this park a few times this year but wasn't sure how Julia would react to off-roading on trails of his comfort level. He had been known to push it a little too far for most normal people.

"What do you think? Wanna start off easy, say on these level one trails marked in green and see how you feel before kicking it up a notch?" The park offered trails for all skill levels from flat, road-like terrain to steep rocky paths that are sure to give a thrill to even the most experienced OHV enthusiast.

"Wow, do I come off as that much of a wimp?" Julia grinned. She grabbed Brad's forearm and laughed when he tried to apologize. "Let's start off on level three and see how I feel before kicking it up a notch."

"That's my girl," Brad reached over, patted her thigh, and gave a mischievous grin. "Julia, my dear, you're in for a treat."

∩∩∩

"THIS PLACE IS FANTASTIC!" Exhilarated, Julia jumped out of the Jeep and spun in a circle as she took in the view. Tall trees grew out of sandy areas and shrubs lined steep hills. Lakes at the bottom of the quarry and sheer cliffs made for breathtaking scenery. "I've never done anything like this before. Thank you for bringing me here. This has been the most fun!"

Off-road machines revved in the distance and Julia smiled at the memory of their day together. She could hardly wait for Brad to get out of the driver's side before she threw her arms around his neck and hugged him tight. When she realized what she was doing, she took a step back. Only after she tilted her chin down then raised her eyes to meet his, did she recognize a longing in

Brad's dark eyes.

Not wanting to let this woman escape, Brad held her around the waist with one arm, his expression serious. He tucked a rogue blonde curl behind her ear, his fingers brushed her cheek then traced the line of her chin. *I must be dreaming*; Brad could not believe such a perfect woman stood so close. Her skin was so soft; the honeysuckle scent of her perfume reached his senses.

Hypnotized by the reflection in his eyes, Julia couldn't look away. She bit her lower lip and reminded herself to breathe. Grasping his arms for support, she stared into his unblinking eyes and whispered, "Brad."

A low groan escaped Brad's throat and he pulled her closer. His lips brushed hers so gently that he wasn't sure if what just happened could be considered a kiss. When he backed away an inch, licked his lips, and focused on Julia's gaze, he promised himself that the next kiss wouldn't be questionable. With a tilt of his head, Brad searched Julia's eyes and found a mirrored passion.

She closed the distance between them, parted her lips, closed her eyes, and finished what he started.

Brad's biceps flexed under her hands as he held her tight. One hand went to the back of her neck to tilt her head so his mouth could cover hers completely. Fingers on his other hand splayed across the small of her back to ensure she stayed close.

Julia's heart raced as their lips and bodies pressed together. All the noise in the background faded away and her body reacted almost on its own. She surprised herself when one hand rested on the back of Brad's neck and the other wrapped around his shoulders. This was the first time she could remember actually losing herself in a kiss. *Nothing beats a first kiss.*

They broke the connection but remained in the embrace. Although they both fought to catch their breath, smiles spread wide across their faces.

"Wow, Julia." Brad exhaled.

"Yeah. Me too." Julia kept her eyes closed; she didn't want to come back to reality. Not yet. A kiss on her nose broke the spell and she opened her eyes to find Brad staring at her.

"Hungry?" he asked and she nodded.

The pavilion area offered several tables, but one had been dressed in a white tablecloth prior to the couple's arrival. A basket of food sat in the center and a bottle of wine rested in a metal cooler.

"You had this all planned?" Julia asked, pleasantly surprised. "Dinner complete with a white tablecloth and wine. I'm impressed. Thank you."

A one-shoulder shrug showed Brad's humility.

Once they settled, comfortable conversation flowed. "I found this place after I bought my Jeep. I told you a little about the clubs; I joined the one that the dealership recommended because they were an affiliate. They demanded a certain amount of time and money to be spent and I just didn't have the time, so I dropped it. I'm working on finding more time to do things for me."

"I totally get it, it's so hard to find any time for myself. Today has been exactly what I needed. And this pavilion has the best view, just beautiful," Julia studied the horizon before she fixed her gaze on Brad. A sincere smile reached all the way to her eyes and touched Brad's heart. "I would love to know more about you, Brad. Tell me a little about your family." She opened the Mustcanelli from Marker Cellars Winery and poured it into two plastic glasses.

Brad unpacked the food; sandwich makings wrapped on plastic plates made the perfect dinner for this setting. Turkey, ham, vegetables, dressings, cheeses, and macaroni salad sat between them on the table.

"First, a toast." Brad picked up his glass of wine and tipped it toward Julia. She did the same. "To you, Julia." His eyes twinkled in the sunlight. "Who knew that such a beautiful, smart, independent, successful woman could be so outgoing, adventurous, a little sassy, and a whole lotta sexy." He winked. *Everything I have ever dreamed of in a perfect mate. Damn, she checks every box.* He didn't dare say that out loud but couldn't take his eyes off her.

Speechless, Julia smiled and clinked her glass to his before taking a sip. Once she found her voice, she changed the subject; "Mmm, this wine. Just perfect; light and peachy." After another sip, Julia's shoulders relaxed. She closed her eyes and tilted her head toward the sky. The cadence of Brad's voice brought her back to reality.

"My parents met in 1985 when they were both selected to be in the Blue Bell Ice Cream commercial. It's kind of a big deal in Paradise; that's really the only reason anyone knows the town exists. They were married six months later and had my twin brothers eight months after that. Can't believe they stayed married for thirty years."

After Brad paused and shook his head, Julia hesitated. "Oh, I'm sorry. Did your mom pass away?"

"No," Brad chuckled. "She left. About five years ago now." He looked over Julia's shoulder and wondered if he should tell the entire embarrassing story now or later. *Later.* "I come from a long line of hunters. My grandfather taught my father, who taught my brothers and me everything about hunting. I was always the best at dressing whatever we bagged, so I was permanently assigned the task.

"The rest of the guys would drink and play poker while they waited for me to finish." The passive expression on Julia's face was hard to read. Brad knew she didn't like that he was a butcher but didn't yet know the extent of her dislike for hunters. "I'm dying to learn more about you." He offered a patient grin.

At some point Julia understood she would need to tell her story too, so she figured it would be better to get it all on the table, literally, before they went any further. She could never pinpoint exactly when previous boyfriends got turned off. *Previous boyfriends? Am I seriously thinking that Brad could be boyfriend material? Uh, I'm not so sure about that. Just friends, right?*

Warmth from the wine flushed her cheeks. She hated this part of the first date talk. "My mom had me when she was just eighteen, then my four brothers and sisters in quick succession. I guess you could say we lived on the wrong side of the tracks; never really had much."

She pursed her lips and gauged Brad's interest before continuing. *At least he didn't flinch. Yet.*

"My dad was a hunter, too, but he drank too much and never held a job for long. He didn't go to college, barely graduated from high school, which drove me to be the best I could be to escape that life. Mother stayed with him because she had nowhere else to go. She finally left him after all the kids were grown. My youngest sister is just like my dad; I knew she would be from the time I went to college. She was only twelve and already headed in the wrong direction. But that's a story for a different day."

Memories of Julia's youth had a way of upsetting her and she didn't want to ruin such a beautiful day with Brad, so she asked him another question. "Julia said you went to Texas A&M for a couple years. That was my first choice if I could have gone somewhere out of state. What was your major?"

"You're asking about me?" Brad tilted his head and grinned.

"Of course. I need to know what I'm getting into before I start something. Besides, she obviously told you some things about me. Setting us up has been on her agenda for a year."

"Well." Brad crossed his arms and leaned on the table. "What did she say?" He didn't answer her question.

"Not much, just that you didn't finish, that you came back to start the business."

Brad raised his eyes and smirked at Julia before looking away, almost as if he wanted to say something but held back.

"Brad? Why do you keep smirking at me?"

"I'm not smirking at you." The sound of his name

on her lips was like music.

Julia rolled her eyes and stared across the table at Brad.

"Fine. I smirked. You caught me." A genuine chuckle seemed to relax him even more. Brad tilted his head. "You're just..." Pausing to think of the perfect words, he tapped his lips with his index finger, squinted, and grinned. "Lanie tried to explain how you would be so perfect for me, but she didn't get it quite right."

A V formed between Julia's eyebrows. "Because?"

"She didn't tell me that you are gorgeous at 4am wearing an old MSU T-shirt with your hair pulled back and just as striking sitting at this table having dinner with a new friend."

Julia bit her lower lip and Brad's eyes grew dark. Without breaking their shared gaze, she confirmed, "A new friend."

∩∩∩

DOGS BARKED IN THE kennel and a boarded bird shrieked in the reception area, forcing Julia to break the passionate kiss and release her arms from around Brad's neck. The exam table, hard and cold under her thighs, proved to be an inconvenient area for getting close to her so-called "new friend." With her hands on Brad's chest and his lips tracing her chin, Julia groaned as she moved her hands to his cheeks. She placed a short kiss on his lips, smiled, and nudged him from his place between her knees. "Follow me," she whispered.

The white, tailless cat stared at Brad as he helped Julia off the table. "That's creepy," he said more to himself than to Julia.

"Hey, Peanut." Julia laughed as her hand stroked the cat's fur. She walked out the back door, locked it behind Brad, and grabbed his hand. They strolled the short distance to Julia's house and she turned to him before opening the door. "Come in for a drink?"

Darkness reached Brad's eyes and a grin formed on his lips.

Julia chuckled. "Just one. Just a drink. I don't want this perfect day to end quite yet."

Rustic River Ranch

Saturday, July 11, 2020

RANDOM BOTTLES OF wine sat in metal coolers in the middle of a round table at the Marker Cellars Winery. After a busy week, the wedding party, now close friends, met up for a mutual date. They returned to the beloved wedding venue to celebrate Max and Lanie as newlyweds and say goodbye to Sarah and Jared before they left for their home states.

The owners, Mark and Becky, pulled up chairs and chatted about the wedding the previous weekend. "We enjoyed your families and friends so much. It was a beautiful day, just the perfect day, and we feel so honored that you choose to be married here." Becky smiled at Max.

Mark said to Lanie, "The reception was so fun, the music y'all chose and the DJ just livened this place up. Not to mention when the band was called on stage. We never tire of the shenanigans of wedding receptions. Each one is always so different."

A laugh from Jared made everyone turn their heads. "How about Max's cousin tripping over his own feet as he tried to catch the garter?" He slapped his knee. "I've never seen someone literally swim in the air, or a better save. Man, that would have hurt if he fell."

"And your dad, Lanie? Spilling his cider on that little kid." Sarah shook her head and chuckled. "Oh, my god, I thought he was going to start rolling on the floor he was laughing so hard."

Pam lifted her glass of wine in a toast. "To Max and Lanie." Everyone else lifted their glasses and Pam continued. "Here's to a life full of love and laughter, new adventures, and old friends."

"Hear, hear!" the group said in unison.

"And here's to finding new love." Lanie nodded to Sarah and Jared, who were sitting so close to each other that the resident cat had a hard time getting between them.

"And to finding new friends." Max winked at Brad, who did his best to look nonchalant.

"Y'all coming back to my place for a bonfire?" Brad offered. "I've made arrangements for everyone to have a room."

METAL AND WOOD formed an arch that stretched high above the driveway that led to Brad's property. As they drove under it, Julia read the words carved between the metal frame. "Rustic River Ranch. That sounds inviting."

"My dad never named this place the entire time he owned it." Parking in his driveway to wait for the rest of the convoy, Brad met Julia's eyes. "When I took over, my whole point was to revive the land, the brand, the philosophy. A new start for everyone. For everything." He paused for a moment, then admitted, "I feel really lucky to be able to spend time with you two nights in a row. I'm so glad this get-together was already planned; I don't know what I would do if I had to wait an entire week to spend another evening with you. I'm infatuated, Julia. You are..." Brad sighed and stopped before he made a fool of himself. What was he thinking admitting how he felt so quickly after their first date?

Picking up on his hesitation, Julia felt the need to express her feelings too. " I'm glad we're able to spend more time together too. I almost hate to admit that I missed you today. I haven't had a connection with anyone in so long, I almost forgot what it's like."

Brad placed a quick kiss on Julia's lips and laughed at her surprise. "Come on, I know you want to see Charlie."

Two steps led to a wrap-around porch with rocking chairs on either side of a decorative entrance door. Etched glass filled the center of a white door which was framed by the brick house. Once inside, Brad led Julia to a room on the left. "This used to be the family room, but it's Charlie's room now. That crate was too small for him, so I cleared out most of the furniture in here."

A TV hung on one wall and a small mattress sat against the opposite wall. "He gets to watch cartoons all day? What a spoiled kid," Julia teased, sitting next to Charlie on the mattress; she ran her hand along the soft fur on his head. Charlie wagged his tail and leaned into Julia's touch. "Hey, boy. How are you? Your new daddy taking good care of you?"

"New daddy? You haven't found his owners?" Brad's eyes widened hopefully.

"Well, it's been a week. I usually give two weeks before clearing an animal for adoption, but with Charlie's level of malnutrition, there's no doubt he was a drop-off. I'll have you sign some paperwork that'll legally make him yours. The language covers the unlikely event of the so-called owners coming back and trying to claim him. Not going to happen; I'll be more than happy to testify in court if it comes to that."

"Wow, that's great news. Thank you, sweetheart."

In full doctor mode, it had been easier to dismiss the unexpected but welcomed term of endearment. Julia smiled as she checked over the dog's injured areas. "The sutures are holding up nicely, and Charlie seems to be in good spirits. He's getting up to potty okay?"

"He needed help for the first few days, but he's learned just how much weight he can put on the one leg. He's doing well. Besides, Sherri, my sister-in-law, comes over three times a day to check on him and I spend most of my time in here when I'm home." When he noticed Julia trying to hide a smile, he shrugged. "He needs the company. We like it. Not to mention," Brad grinned at the gorgeous blonde sitting beside *his* dog and added, "he has the best, most loving doctor a dog could ask for."

Julia reached her hand out toward Brad and he helped her stand. Once on her feet, he pulled her into his arms. "The most loving person anyone could ask for."

A blush reached Julia's cheeks and she glanced away.

"I mean it." Brad tilted her chin so he could look into her eyes; she didn't have a chance to evade his comment a second time. "The most loving person." He lowered his head and touched his lips to hers, parting them for a deep kiss. Just as their hands began to roam, a truck honked in the driveway.

An overexaggerated groan escaped Brad and he pressed his forehead to hers. "To be continued." He smiled as his lips touched hers again.

∩∩∩

BRAD GRABBED HIS keys and cowboy hat before leading Julia out the door. Coolers filled with ice and cups lined the sidewalk and firewood sat neatly stacked on the far side of the driveway in front of three side-by-side ATVs.

Julia had promised herself that this night was all about celebrating Lanie and Max and opening her mind to new possibilities. She would relax, sit back, and let whatever was supposed to happen, happen.

Every aspect of her work life had been controlled, which made it easier to keep up with her patients' needs; her personal life easily followed suit and she hoped to change that. At least a little.

After the supplies had been loaded, the four couples packed in the ATVs and began the drive through half a mile of trails to Brad's favorite spot on his property. Natural landscape flagstone lined a fire pit between two cabins that sat adjacent to a six-acre pond. Tall trees provided shade during the day but at night, the moon could still shine through.

Bottles of wine and cans of cider and beer littered a picnic table in front of one of the cabins. A fire roared to life in the pit soon after the friends chose their poisons and settled in chairs close enough to revel in the heat.

"Lanie and I had been planning that day for a year. There was no detail that we hadn't gone over a thousand times. There was no way to mess it up. No way," Max had been dying to tell his friends details of the "cake" story since the wedding. "I have never been so nervous in front of a crowd, though. I was standing in front of all the guests and praying that I wouldn't screw up the vows.

"My dad asked how I was holding up, I looked at my granny, she waved at me from the front row, and I knew everything would be perfect. I told my dad I was good, excited, then I closed my eyes for a second and took a deep breath to relax. I heard my dad say, 'Once you say, 'I do' the rest is cake.'" My eyes shot open and I swear I yelled, 'Oh shit. The cake. Dad. I forgot to bring the cake.'"

Laughter reverberated between the trees and across the pond. Max had a way of setting the scene and his facial expressions had the entire group wrapped up in his story.

Lanie took over reminiscing. "I heard from the

photographer already. There are some exceptional pictures and some hilarious pictures. One, specifically, is of Julia and Brad."

Surprised, Julia's eyebrows lifted. "Really? Hilarious how?"

"During the wedding party portraits." Lanie paused, closed her eyes, and chuckled. "You're sneering at Brad and Brad is cracking up. It's the best, I swear. What was that all about?"

"Oh, that." Julia pursed her lips and nudged Brad. "Go ahead, tell them what you said to me."

"Come on, it was a good joke." Brad raised his eyebrows and waited for her to agree. When Julia continued to stare back at him, straight-faced, he gave in. "Fine. I said that I overheard two blondes talking in the grocery store the other day. The first one said that her boyfriend was a veterinarian, the other one asked, 'Oh, did he fight in a war?' She responded with, 'No, you dumbass, he doesn't eat meat.'"

Sarah spit the wine out of her mouth into the fire and everyone else erupted in laughter.

After Lanie caught her breath, she said, "That's the exact moment that the photographer snapped the picture."

Brad put his arm around Julia's shoulders and pulled her close. "Admit it. That was funny." He placed a kiss in her hair. His cowboy hat hovered above her head, and the scent of his cologne lingered until he backed away.

Lanie caught Julia's eye and winked at the intimate gesture before raising her glass in a silent *you go, girl.*

"Fine, it was funny." Dizzy from the moment, not the wine, Julia couldn't stop smiling. She made it a point to only have one drink to ensure that her decisions remained sincere. She noticed that Brad was still on his first drink too.

"This place is fantastic, Brad," Pam said after the laughter died down and everyone else's glasses had been replenished. Then she asked the question that's been on Julia's mind for a week. "I have to ask. How do you do it?"

Confused, Brad squinted at Pam. "Do what?"

"How do you kill animals for a living?"

"Wow, Pam." Jason nudged his wife and scowled. "Nothing like putting a guy on the spot,"

"Well..." Brad shrugged. It was obvious that he had been asked this question numerous times and had worked out the perfect response. "The simple answer is that people have to eat. Look, I know that sounds harsh, but I really am an animal lover. I went to A&M for two years with the intention of being a veterinarian." A glance at Julia told him that Lanie hadn't told her that part of his story; her eyes widened and she tiled her head.

"I excelled in chemistry, biology, and physics, but when it came to world history, poly sci, literature, and fine arts, I got bored. Besides, all my family and friends already depended on me to process their livestock at a reasonable economical fee, so I came home and opened the shop."

A new understanding of the man that sat beside her brought a grin to Julia's lips. This added a level of depth to her new friend that she hadn't expected. She tilted her head and studied Brad's profile. *Gorgeous, smart, funny, sexy; oh, my god, that cowboy hat. He's successful, an animal and outdoor lover; what else could I possibly want in a man? He must have such a hard heart, though, to fully process those animals.* Still unsure if she wanted to let her feelings flow, Julia guarded her heart. *Would he soften to his woman? Would he be able to love me like I've always wanted?*

Satisfied with Brad's answer, Jason turned toward Max. "My favorite part of the reception was when everyone begged Max to play. Not only did you oblige, you and Jared rocked the house. I haven't ever been much of a country music fan, but since you sang the song you wrote and dedicated to your bride, I'm hooked. The passion and meaning behind the words really touched me. Who knew that real people actually wrote those songs? It just hit home, man."

"Thanks, Jason. That's really great to hear. It means so much when I get that kind of feedback." Max shot a look at Jared and he nodded before letting go of Sarah's hand to stand. "We have a surprise for y'all."

The two guitar players strummed out a few songs around the fire and Brad joined in the harmonizing. Sarah was mesmerized and practically drooled as she watched Jared play with his friends. Julia closed her eyes and reveled in the glorious sounds of the men's voices as they sang. They warmed up with a couple cover songs and Brad's first hit, "Texas Summer Nights," before playing a newly written original.

"This one's for the love of my life, I call it Blind Faith." Max blew a kiss to Lanie, tipped his hat, and began to hum.

> *Sitting in this hotel bar, you're a*
> *million miles away*
> *The guys in the band are surrounded*
> *by pretty girls*
> *Dressed in short skirts, heels, and*
> *strings of pearls*
> *I realize I'll never be alone; You're*
> *all I can see*
> *And I'm so thankful that our love is*

strong

There's no way anyone could ever

come between us

Loving you is easy; it's you and me

baby

It's you and me baby; it's us against

the world

Because you have blind faith in me

Laughter surrounds me, giggles

laced with wine

Blondes, brunettes, and redheads,

women of all kinds

I don't see them, I don't care

You're the only one on my mind

And you'll be here all night

There's no way anyone could ever

come between us

It's you and me baby; it's us against

the world

Our love is so true; it's you and me

baby

Because you have blind faith in me

∩∩∩

MURMURS FROM INSIDE each of the cabins reached

Brad and Julia as they readied the side-by-side for the drive back to the house. "Where did Sarah and Jared go?" The ATV on the far side of the cabin roared to life and Jared shushed Sarah's giggles. "Never mind," Julia grinned and fastened her seatbelt.

As they followed tree-lined trails back to the house, the hum of the machine lulled Julia into a fantasy. She allowed herself to envision living on a property so expansive. There were so many activities that they could do all without leaving their own yard, so to speak. Fishing, camping, riding trails, hiking, watching wildlife, exploring new areas, and creating their own intimate go-to spaces.

Wait, Julia. Don't get so ahead of yourself. What's with all this "they" and "their"? I'm starting to sound like life might welcome me on this property. I barely know Brad. But, God, he's sexy. The way he kisses me, mmm. She closed her eyes and for a second, she swore she could feel the heat of his hands as they moved all over her body and warmed her skin.

A tree root jolted the ATV and Julia back to reality. The house was within sight and she tried not to plan what might happen next. Once they parked in the circular drive by the front steps, Brad turned in the seat to face Julia. His cowboy hat sat low on his brow, stirring an attraction that Julia fought to control.

Brad traced the line of Julia's chin with his fingers, giving her chills. She smiled and tilted her head in anticipation of his full lips touching hers. He gazed into her eyes as if teasing her; he knew she wanted this kiss just as much as he did. "My god, Julia," he breathed.

Warmth spread throughout her body before he even kissed her. When his hand moved under her hair and steadied her neck, her breathing increased, and lips parted. The instant his mouth covered hers, Julia closed her eyes and found herself concentrating on the way his touch filled her with desire. As if moving without instruction, one hand found Brad's face and the other wrapped around his shoulders.

"Brad..." Deep breaths consumed them both; Julia shook her head at the same time Brad nodded. Genuine laughs mixed as they rush to exit the side-by-side.

Hand-in-hand, they reached the front door; Brad paused to glance at Julia and smiled. His perfectly straight teeth gleamed in the dim porch lights. He wrapped one arm around her waist and pulled her to him.

As much as she told herself it would be a bad idea to go inside, she refused to resist. She rested her arms over his shoulders and waited. Brad leaned forward, pulled her closer, and kissed her nose. She giggled as she acknowledged that their bodies touched from chest to knee. *Damn it, I don't want to stop.*

When the door closed behind Julia, Brad pushed her up against it, the force of his body trapped her in place. She gasped and her hands instinctively gripped the waist of his jeans making sure he didn't back away. Brad's eyes darkened with longing as he put one hand on the door beside her head and the other gripped the back of her neck. His lips covered hers and he breathed his passion into her.

Julia absorbed his desire as if he was breathing a new life into her soul. She matched his every move and pressed her body into to his as if she demanded to be satisfied. The last time she'd felt this type of natural, animalistic attraction to anyone was...well, never.

He groaned as he released her mouth and planted hot kisses on her neck. His hands moved from her throat to her breast, causing a whimper to escape as she clung to him.

"Julia…" Heavy breaths jointed wet kisses from her chin to her mouth. "Jesus, you're driving me crazy." Brad held her to him and searched her eyes for a sign that she wanted this just as much as he did. When she smiled and initiated the next deep kiss, he didn't hesitate to lift her off her feet and carry her to his bed.

BRAD CLUNG TO JULIA as if his next breath depended on her body remaining tangled with his. "I've been looking for you my entire life."

She ran her fingers through his thick dark hair and whispered, "I'm right here."

Walking Beam Brewery

Tuesday, July 14, 2020

CLOUDS SEEMINGLY lifted Julia off the ground as she floated through the clinic. While she performed her morning surgery prep routine, Teri had busied herself with restocking shelves. Country music played in the background and filled the air with pleasant but distracting noise.

Max's song "Texas Summer Nights" came on and Teri started to sing along. "The sound of crickets and owls fills the dark, Life is so much sweeter with Lanie by my side." She caught Julia's eye and said, "How cool is it that you're friends with Max Walker? Max Walker!" One hand covered her chest and she drew in a deep, dreamy breath before she raised her eyes to the heavens. "I'm so jealous."

"If you want to meet him, Teri, I can hook you up."

With a wink Julia added, "I got a guy," in her best Jersey accent. The ladies laughed as bells rang above the door—a suggestion that they should behave and act more professional.

One of Julia's long-time friends-turned-client, Jennifer Nelson, carried a lilac British Shorthair kitten in one arm like a movie star would a Yorkie. "Hey girls," she sang her hello and sat her purse on the counter. "I need shots and a neuter for this guy before he goes to his new family. You know, the usual. The works."

Paperwork attached to a clipboard had been placed in front of Jennifer on the counter. "Just need his name and signature. Your signature, not his." Teri laughed at her own joke. "How ya been, Jen?"

"Great, Teri, thanks. But not as great as Julia, apparently. She's floating," The kitten crawled from Jennifer's arms to the counter and began to groom himself.

"Always so observant, aren't you? You could read me like a book from the day we met." Julia tried to hide a smile but failed. "You're going to ask, so I might as well tell you. Yes, I met someone. We've gone out a couple times and..." She raised one shoulder and turned her smile to the ground.

"And? Come on, Jules, spill." Impatient, Jennifer stood with her hands on her hips and tapped her foot for effect.

"And nothing. It's nothing." Julia rolled her eyes and knew both of her friends saw through her. "Fine. We met up with Lanie and Max's wedding party at the winery Saturday night. We all went back to Brad's place to hang out around a bonfire and..." Heat from the memory of the way Brad took control the minute they walked in the house rose from Julia's neck to her cheeks. "He is the best kisser, I swear. And the way he looked at me, touched me, whispered sweet nothings in my ear after we..." She closed her eyes and smiled.

"Mmm, hmm. Good for you, girlfriend." Jennifer winked at Teri.

Julia grinned. "He's exactly what I've been looking for my entire life. Except one thing."

An exaggerated sigh and a groan from Teri made Jennifer chuckle as she said, "Yeah, there's always just one thing. What's so wrong with this guy that he's not good enough?"

Julia squinted more inwardly at herself than at Jennifer and wondered if that's how every man in her life had been dismissed. *Not good enough.* "He's a butcher," she admitted.

"Oh, you mean the Daniels guy? Dude, jackpot!" Jennifer smiled and nodded. "He's frickin' hot. Have you seen him?" She paused and tilted her head. "Wait a minute. I have; just saw him last night, as a matter of fact. Are y'all exclusive?"

"What do you mean you saw him?" Julia turned to face Jennifer. "He told me he couldn't see me because he was meeting with a potential client in Loving last night. And yes, we are exclusive." A glance between Teri and Jennifer made Julia anxious. "What's going on, Jen?"

"Well, I was at the Walking Beam in Bridgeport having dinner...Have you been there, yet? Oh, my god, the Hawaiian pizza on a cauliflower crust is to die for. They have a great selection of craft beer too..."

"Jen." Julia stepped closer and grabbed her friend's forearm. "Come on, girl. Focus,"

Wide-eyed, Jennifer continued. "Well, your *Brad* was a little on the tipsy side, to say the least, and got into it with the waitress. He made a pretty big scene. Something about the beer not being cold enough, or it not being served in a frosted mug. I don't know, he was just being a loud ass. And that girl he was with looked like a streetwalker, I swear. Doubtful that she was a 'potential client'," Jennifer used finger quotes, "unless Brad's into some other business that this town isn't aware of."

"He was with a girl?" Julia froze. The part about him causing a scene was secondary to him being with someone else. She didn't want to hear that the man she thought was so right for her had been with another girl. Not again. Making sure she heard correctly and understood the implications, she repeated the phrase. "That looked like a streetwalker?" It came out as a whisper. *What is it with my taste in men? Does everyone cheat?*

"Boobs"—Jennifer held her hands six inches from her own ample chest—"out to here. Fake, for sure. You know those girls that wear a black bra with the lace hanging out under a white, super-wide U-neck tank top? Yeah, that's really not a good look." She turned her head and made a face at Teri. "Big blonde hair, four-inch heels. She kept saying, 'Come on, baby, let's just go.' When she stood to follow him out, I swear you could see under-cheek, her skirt was so short. She was definitely wearing a thong. Definitely."

"Jesus, Jen. Sometimes you just need to keep your trap shut." Teri threw daggers in support of Julia and began processing paperwork for the kitten's surgery.

"No, Teri. I need to hear this. Thanks, but I need to know sooner rather than later if this guy is just another lying, unfaithful, asshole. Nothing like finding out three years into a relationship, like last time." Julia leaned against the counter, tilted her head back, and sighed. "Damn it. I really liked him."

A text message alert in the form of a muffled meow

came from Jennifer's purse as she was signing the surgery form. She read the text then looked at her watch before nodding at Teri. "I gotta run. See you around six?"

"We close at five." Teri smiled and added, "You're so lucky Doc loves you."

With a nod and a wave, Jennifer pushed through the door.

$$\cap\cap\cap$$

DURING THE MORNING spay and neuter surgeries, Julia's mind wandered to the earlier conversation with Jennifer. It had been difficult to ignore the image she created of Brad accompanied by a woman dressed in a revealing top and short skirt, as he made a scene at the Walking Beam restaurant. *What was I thinking? I shouldn't have let myself believe that there was room for a relationship in my life, anyway. My patients need me more than I need some jerk that's only going to break my heart. It's just not worth it.*

For lunch, Teri bought salads from the Finish Line Café and Julia nibbled at hers between checking on the recovering cats and dogs housed in the kennel. Her mind had been clouded with doubt as she picked apart every compliment from Brad and each word that he had whispered in her ear as they made love.

Luck was on Julia's side when none of her clients demanded to discuss their bill or needed confirmation on after-care for their pet. She could hardly speak a full sentence, let alone focus on details beyond her typical daily routine. Teri had checked on her throughout the day and asked if she wanted to talk. Of course, she didn't; her thoughts hadn't been organized enough to speak them aloud. Yet.

At five o'clock, Teri shut down her computer and began her cleaning duties. Five minutes later, the bells above the door chimed; the office was never locked until the doctor was ready to leave for the day just in case a client ran a little late. Like Jennifer.

From the back room, Julia heard Teri's tone but not the words she spoke. Footsteps proceeded the vet tech into the kennel. "Julia." When she didn't respond, Teri repeated louder, "Julia. He's here."

"Who, Teri?" Annoyed, Julia's tone fell flat.

"Brad. And he looks so good. Very happy. All smiles. You need to check yourself before you come out, ok?" Nodding toward the bathroom, Teri made her way back to the lobby.

Blonde curls frizzed like a halo around Julia's reflection in the mirror. The crease above her eyebrows, frown on her lips, and pale complexion made Julia gasp at the unexpected sight. *Thank you, Teri.* After she crunched her curls with wet hands, added a layer of powder and a bit of eyeliner, Julia put on a fake smile and rechecked her appearance. *Good enough.*

Teri was right; Brad had always been striking in that black felt cowboy hat. After the way she gushed about how much she loved it on Friday night, she had a feeling he wore it just for her. When he saw Julia, a smile formed on his lips and stretched from ear to ear; the sincerity reached his eyes. He greeted Julia with a colorful bouquet of summer flowers and leaned in to kiss her on the cheek. "Hey, beautiful. I missed you."

As she backed away from his attempted embrace, he narrowed his eyes and reached for her hand. "I just now got home. Actually, I haven't even been home yet. I came straight here. I couldn't stand another minute without seeing your face."

Julia turned her back to him, shook her head, and let out a barely audible scoff.

"Julia, what's going on? Is everything ok?"

Turning to face him, she crossed her arms over her chest and lifted her chin. "Where were you last night?"

Still holding the flowers, his smile faded. "I spent the night in Loving. Like I told you, I had a meeting with a potential business partner—Jason Payne, Pam's husband. What's this all about?" Brad frowned and laid the flowers on the counter.

"My friend saw you having dinner with a scantily clad woman at a restaurant in Bridgeport." Julia decided to keep the explanation short and sweet.

"What?" Two steps narrowed the distance between them. Brad needed to understand what exactly Julia was insinuating. "That's not possible. I was in Loving. Jason offered me a room; I didn't even stay in a hotel." He reached for Julia's hand. "You have to believe me. After the night we shared and the promise we made to be exclusive—I would never break that promise. I would never do anything to hurt you, Julia. I don't know who your friend saw, but it wasn't me."

When Julia's cold gaze didn't falter, Brad backed away and shook his head. He lifted his hat to run his hand through his hair. He squinted his eyes and focused on the tiled floor. Lifting his gaze to Julia, he said, "Get your friend to come over."

"Now?"

"Now. We need to figure this out. I can assure you, the man she saw wasn't me."

As Julia strode toward the desk to reach the office phone, bells rang above the door.

Jennifer stopped before completely crossing the threshold and the door hit her backside. "Oh, shit. What did I just walk into?"

"Ah, Jen. Perfect timing, as always." Julia kept a straight face and didn't answer her friend's question. Instead, she let Jennifer come to her own conclusion.

"Boy, the tension in here is thick enough to cut with a knife. And what are you doing here?" With a furrowed brow, she addressed the man that stood in the middle of the waiting room. "Brad, is it? After I told Julia what I witnessed last night, I'm surprised she let you through the door."

"Pardon me, ma'am, but I've never seen you in my life. I have no idea what you're talking about."

Not one to sugarcoat any discussion, Jennifer let Brad have a piece of her mind, "of course, you didn't see me, you were too busy bitching out a waitress because your beer wasn't cold enough. The shape you were in when you left Walking Beam, I'm surprised you didn't kill yourself, and that hooker that was with you, on your drive home." Each word dripped more disdain than the previous one.

"Jen..." Julia attempted to calm the situation.

"You shouldn't even give this asshat the time of day, Julia. Someone as two-faced as this guy doesn't deserve you. If he can be with you one minute and a jezebel the next and deny it as if nothing even happened, you need to break it off before you really get your heart stomped on."

KRISTI COPELAND

"You know what?" Brad raised both hands, palms out, and stepped back. "All y'all are just too much. I think everyone needs to walk away before shit really hits the fan." With a slight shake of his head, Brad exhaled and turned to Julia. She allowed him to get close enough so Jen couldn't overhear his words.

"Obviously, this isn't working out well for me. Whoever your friend saw, it wasn't me, I promise you. I hope we can revisit this later," Brad's voice and gaze softened. "I honestly did miss you, Julia; couldn't wait to see you again. I'm sorry this misunderstanding happened. Let me know when you're ready to talk, preferably in private. You have my number."

∩∩∩

LAW AND ORDER played on the television that hung on the opposite wall from the mattress on the floor. A cable station had started running a marathon four hours prior. Charlie's head rested in Brad's lap; his tail wagged as Brad mindlessly stroked his soft fur. Voices coming from the TV provided background noise as Brad's mind wandered. He focused on the conversation he had earlier with Julia and tried his best to figure out what had happened. He had so many questions and had been determined to find answers.

What the hell happened? Why hasn't she called me yet? Will she ever speak to me again? Does she care about me as much as I care for her? We had such a magical night; I truly thought I had finally found a woman that checks every single box of my definition of perfection. Who did Julia's friend see that looked so much like me that she thought she was talking to that very person when I showed up at the clinic? I get it that she believed her friend over me, but... Brad sighed and let that thought trail off as he leaned his head against the wall.

We've only known each other for a couple weeks, maybe it's better to just let it go. Who knows, she may end up changing after six months and leave anyway. Better to get it over with now instead of investing all kinds of time and emotion just to end up with a broken heart. Again.

Charlie whimpered, which brought Brad back to reality. "What's up, bud? Need to go outside?" The dog let out a playful growl and bounded off the bed. Brad lifted himself off the mattress and chuckled. "Okay, okay, I'm coming. Hold your horses."

As Brad waited for his dog to do his business in the fenced backyard, he pulled his phone out of his pocket and dialed his brother's number. "Hey, Greg. You have a minute?"

AMBER LIQUID SWIRLED around ice cubes as Brad tilted the short, thick glass from side to side. "Greg?" Brad addressed his brother with squinted eyes. "Can I ask you a question?"

"I thought that's why you came over." Greg chuckled but his little brother's expression didn't change.

Leaning forward with his forearms resting on his knees, Brad asked, "When you and Sherri started dating, did she ever not believe something you told her? A story or an experience from your past?"

"I'm not exactly sure where you're going with this, but to answer your question, no. She believed every word I ever said. We've known each other since grade school; she knew I was as honest as they come, sometimes to a fault. What's going on, Brad? What's bothering you?"

Crickets chirped in the darkness beyond the wraparound deck of Greg and Sherri's house. Three barn cats stretched along the railing and pretended not to pay attention to the humans.

After Brad's thoughts had been organized, he laid them out for Greg. "I told you about the plans for Saturday night with Max and Lanie's wedding party at the winery. We all ended up back at the ranch and spent a couple hours hanging out at the cabins. Julia stayed that night and we really connected. She continues to amaze me; she's everything I've been searching for."

Unsure how his brother would react to that statement, he glanced over and almost laughed at Greg's jaw hanging open. "Yeah, I know, cheesy, but it's true. You also know that I went to Loving and met with Jason Payne yesterday. The minute I got home, today, I stopped by Julia's clinic. I couldn't wait to see her again, brought flowers and everything. Well, I was pretty much ambushed the minute I walked in the door. I'm so confused." A deep sigh released some tension in Brad's shoulders and he hung his head.

"Explain ambushed," Greg said, trying to understand.

Still focused on the ground, Brad's voice was low. "Julia's friend told her that she saw me with some cheap-looking woman at the Walking Beam Brewery in Bridgeport last night. Obviously, that's impossible because I was meeting with Jason about partnering with his bison ranch." Brad sipped the whiskey and enjoyed the burn as it flowed down his throat.

"She must have been mistaken; just saw someone that looks like you. Maybe you can have Julia ask her friend to meet with you—"

Brad interrupted. "That's the shitty part of this entire story. Her friend actually walked through the door when I was standing there. The second she saw me, she said, 'Oh, shit'. She swore it was me that she saw at the restaurant. What am I going to do to convince her that it wasn't me? I'm stumped."

"Wow," Greg paused to process the information. "I haven't seen you fret over a girl like this since..." He paused again, trying to remember the name of the girl that broke his brother's heart in college.

"Please don't say her name out loud. Just thinking about that mistake makes me shudder."

"No worries, bro. I don't even remember it. What I do remember is that you were so hurt. She said she needed to find someone who could give her more attention and focus on her dreams. What a tool. Obviously, she wasn't the right girl for you."

"No kidding. She didn't want me to hang out with my friends if she wasn't able to, which was never. She tried to control what clothes I wore and refused to let me wear a cowboy hat. And forget about my dream of starting a veterinary business, her dream of working at her father's law firm outweighed anything I cared about." Brad closed his eyes and shook his head, "tell me again why you brought her into this? No, never mind. Don't. I'm not here to talk about the past. I need to know what to do about my future."

Absorbed with his vision of Julia, Brad didn't focus on choosing the right words like he usually did around Greg. His brother had a knack for picking out the slightest insinuation based on a person's body language, tone of voice, and specific phrases.

"You think Julia is your future?"

"What?" Brad pursed his lips and cleared his throat. "Hmm. Maybe I do. I don't have to tell you that she's gorgeous, anyone can see that. It's the little things that she probably doesn't even think about that have a hold on me. She's kind, honest, sincere, hardworking, successful, independent.

"She has a certain air of confidence, like she can take on the world without any help. She's adventurous. Will try almost anything. Our backgrounds are somewhat similar; her father was an avid hunter and her mother stayed home and raised the kids. Her parents are divorced, so she understands what it's like to choose your words carefully around family.

"She makes me feel important, like what I think matters. Not to mention our chemistry." Brad smirked to himself as he remembered how she looked laying in his bed covered by only a sheet. "She is exactly the kind of woman that I've been dreaming about since I realized I wanted to have a family. Her love for animals alone shows me that she'll be a great mom. Loving, kind, but firm. You should see her with Charlie; she loves that dog almost as much as I do."

"Well, it sounds to me like you've finally found your person. My simple yet sincere advice is that you need to fight for her." Greg's eyebrows raised as he waited for Brad to understand. "If she's not going to call you, you need to call her. Right now."

Brotherly Love

HOGS SQUEALED IN crowded holding pens as Brad set up and organized the cleaning stations and tools before getting to work. Through trial and error, he found that the best way to get out of his own head while he processed animals was to listen to music. Earbuds served a dual purpose, drowning out the sound of the animal while pumping music into his ears. Country music provided the best escape because he could relate to the realism of the lyrics.

After he completed the preparation, Brad took a minute to clear his mind. He sat in an office chair, closed his eyes, and leaned his head back. Instead of the usual white room that entered his mind, a pretty young lady with long, curly blonde hair and warm blue eyes appeared.

Why hasn't Julia called me back? I truly want a

chance to figure this out; I know now that she's the one for me. Once we clicked, our fire burned so hot. Everything about her feels comfortable and right. If she won't answer a voicemail or a text, I need to go see her.

If he didn't block Julia from his mind, he wouldn't accomplish anything today. There was too much to do to allow stray thoughts. Brad stood, positioned himself in front of the big table, picked up one of his tools, and turned up the volume on his earbuds. Startled by a hand on his shoulder, Brad dropped the clever on the stainless steel table. "Jesus, Greg!" As he turned and removed his earbuds, the stern expression on his brother's face gave him pause. "I could have cut off something that I would like to keep attached."

Unfazed by his little brother's harsh tone, Greg said, "You need to come into the store. Right now."

∩∩∩

SHELVES STOCKED WITH unique local food items—jellies and jams, spices and sauces, and dehydrated fruit and jerky—stood on one side of the entrance door and the checkout counter on the other side.

An older, heavier version of Brad with thick gray hair stood behind the register with his arms crossed and lips pursed. Julia stopped mid-stride when, beyond the jerky cooler, Brad spoke to a short, chesty woman in a skimpy leather skirt. In her fantasy, Brad would only ever refer to her or their future children as "baby".

An unusual sinking feeling in her stomach left a frown on Julia's face; she wasn't used to this sensation. Red flags had been an easy way for her to break up with previous boyfriends before she cared enough to be jealous. Once a cheater, always a cheater. Unfortunately, her father had been the first person to prove that statement; her ex-fiancé the most recent.

In Julia's previous life, she would have walked away without confronting the man who had wronged her. After the last time her heart had been broken, she made a promise that she would stand up for herself if it ever happened again. Even though she had high hopes for a relationship with Brad, the doubt of letting herself completely fall in love for someone who killed and butchered animals had never really left her mind.

After Julia took a deep breath to ready herself, she stepped forward. "So." Everyone turned their attention to her as she made her presence known. "You were at the Walking Beam Brewery on Monday."

"What if I was?" Brad found Julia at the edge of the store and glared. His tone was unlike anything she remembered—ugly and mean. "What's it to you?"

Stunned and unsure what to say exactly, Julia spit

out the first thing that came to mind, "Jen was right about you. I deserve better. I can't believe I wasted my time." She turned to leave, but before she made it to the door, a familiar voice caught her attention and made her stop.

"Tracey?" Brad and his older brother, Greg, emerged from the side door. Julia watched as two versions of the same man faced each other. "What the hell are you doing here? What do you want?"

Oh, shit. What the...? Julia thought. She couldn't believe her eyes. The men looked exactly the same, physically, but their stance and air were exactly opposite. *No way. Twins? Brad has a twin?* The real Brad had been focused on the couple at the front of the store, so he hadn't spotted Julia. She couldn't pull herself away from the unbelievable scene if she tried.

"Come on, baby, let's go," the woman whined and reached for Tracey's arm. As she tugged, he pushed her away. She stumbled and giggled while she slurred, "Come on, Trace. That bottle of Cuervo is calling my name."

"Not until I get what I came for." Tracey dismissed the woman, glared at his twin for a moment, then focused on the man behind the counter. "Fifty thousand will work for now. *Dad.*" The last word dripped with sarcasm. "You can get the rest to me later. I'll be around." With an outstretched hand and a smug expression, Tracey waited.

"I don't have that kind of money." Visibly shaken, the older man backed away from the register. He glanced toward Brad and Greg as they approached the counter. Greg gripped Tracey's elbow and forced him toward the exit. "You need to leave, little brother."

Julia moved out of the way and bumped into a display; a jar of jelly fell to the floor and broke. The sound of glass shattering brought Brad's attention to the area.

"Oh, my god. Julia," Brad gasped and raced to where she stood. After he pulled her into his office beyond the shelves, he closed the door and wrapped her in his arms. "I'm so sorry," he whispered in her hair. "I've been trying to call you." Her honeysuckle scent brought back memories of the night they spent together. Each time Brad saw Julia's face, he felt himself falling a little deeper.

Unsure of how she felt about Brad, Julia stiffened when he pulled her close. From what happened in the store, she assumed it was safe to assume he had not, in fact, been the man Jennifer saw at the Walking Beam Brewery. Once she allowed herself to return the embrace, she didn't want to let go. His touch brought a sense of peace and felt like home. As much as she tried to talk herself out of having honest feelings for Brad, he continued to find ways to make it impossible.

Muffled voices from the parking lot stopped as a car started and tires squealed. Brad pulled back, framed her face with his hands, and searched her eyes. "Julia..." He sighed before he placed a brief kiss on her tender lips. "I'm so sorry you had to witness that."

After Julia relaxed, she asked, "Brad, what just happened? Who was that? You have a twin? I'm so confused." She closed her eyes and shook her head as she tried to understand.

If Brad had a choice, the scene between his brothers and his dad would have happened in private. Because Julia had been in the wrong place at the wrong time, Brad decided he needed to explain now. He motioned to the desk chair and Julia lowered herself into it. Leaning against filing cabinets on the adjacent wall, Brad offered a brief explanation.

"I told you I had two brothers, right? Greg is older and Tracey and I are twins. Tracey is basically an outlaw and only comes around when he needs something. He's been in jail for the past four years in Atlanta; I had no idea he had been released. I'm just as confused as you." Julia's blank expression made Brad chuckle. "Well, maybe not just as confused. Look, I need to tell you a really long story, but I have a packed day. Can we please talk about all this later?"

Julia nodded and Brad exhaled a breath he didn't realize he had been holding in anticipation of her response. "Will you come over after you're finished at the clinic?"

∩∩∩

CHARLIE BARKED BEYOND the closed door and Julia smiled at the memory of how Brad cared for the wounded dog. As she stood on the front porch, Julia questioned if she should have come here. *So, he's not a cheater—as far as I know, but is love worth all this drama? Love? Oh, man. Really Julia?* The thought came into her mind before she could make sense of it. Or make it go away.

Julia's heart rate increased the second Brad appeared. *Does he seriously look this hot on purpose or is it just how he is? That damn black cowboy hat...* She smiled as she forced herself to concentrate on breathing and not jumping into his arms, then directly into his bed.

Before he spoke, Brad leaned in, kissed Julia on the cheek, and pulled her into a brief embrace. A muted scent of citrus and rosemary reached Julia's senses; she was proud of herself for refusing to kiss his neck.

Blonde locks pulled into a ponytail were unable to

diminish Julia's beauty in Brad's eyes, even if she did try to downplay her looks. He stepped back for a moment, examined how the white lacy tank top and long flowing skirt simultaneously accentuated and masked her curves and took a deep breath. "God, you're gorgeous."

An eyeroll had always been Julia's go-to expression when someone paid her a compliment. She told herself she needed to work on that, but today was not that day. Blowing off her attraction, Julia commented on how well Charlie was getting around as he pushed himself between them.

"He won't leave me alone until he gets his way, I swear. He must know that I feel sorry for him or something," Brad lead Julia into the kitchen and growled at Charlie. Julia laughed when the dog growled back. "See, we even have our own language. We understand each other."

A basket and a small cooler sat on the counter beside some mail and a glass of water. "You hungry?" Brad asked with raised eyebrows.

Julia nodded. "Can I help you with that?"

"Nope." Brad's attention turned to Charlie. "Go to your room, boy." The dog limped through the door, laid on his bed, and followed Brad's movements with his head as he turned on the TV. "Be back in a little bit. No funny business, mister."

∩∩∩

FISH JUMPED OUT OF the water a few feet from the shore leaving a circular wake as birds chirped in the trees. The summer heat was stagnant without a breeze and Julia fanned herself with one hand, thankful that she wore lightweight clothes. The first time she had been to this area by the lake, three other couples had joined them and helped her relax. This time would be different; Julia hoped there wouldn't be any awkward silence in which her friends could have filled the void, if they were there.

"I have to admit that the past couple of days have been really weird." Brad opened the basket and offered a sandwich to Julia. Two croissants filled with chicken salad had been wrapped in plastic. Potato chips and two bottles of Dos Equis had been placed on the picnic table. "First, seeing you angry broke my heart. The look on your face when you thought I was lying to you—I couldn't get it out of my head."

His eyes met hers from under the low brim of his cowboy hat. "Trying to figure out why your friend thought she saw me with another woman, someone dressed as a harlot at that, was about to drive me crazy. I guess Tracey showing up like he did today has a silver lining. Now you know I was telling the truth about my meeting with Jason in Loving; that's why I couldn't spend time with you. I'm not seeing anyone else, Julia. Don't want to see anyone else. Don't have time to juggle girls, besides that's not my style." Brad laughed, but Julia just popped another chip into her mouth and raised an eyebrow. *She's not going to make this easy.*

He cleared his throat before continuing. "And now you know I have a twin. And he's an ass." Across the table, Julia listened as she devoured the sandwich and washed it down with a sip of cold beer. With a tilt of his head, Brad gazed beyond Julia into the trees and pulled a vision from the depths of his memory. "Tracey and I couldn't have been any different as kids. He was always doing something stupid or careless to get in trouble and I was the one to take the blame. Every time. Even the simplest things like leaving the gate open had huge consequences.

"As you can imagine, a cattle farmer would never leave a gate open." Brad shook his head. "Of course, Tracey blamed me. I had been in the barn napping with Hunter but couldn't prove it. My dad chapped my ass after he and the neighbors finished herding over a hundred head back to our property."

When Julia gasped, Brad's attention turned to her and he blinked away the vision. "You know how they say twins are somehow connected and can feel the same things as if they're almost the same person?" Brad shook his head. "Yeah, not so much. We are identical twins, but the only thing identical about us is our appearance.

"According to court documents, Tracey stole some drug dealer's Camaro and almost killed a guy when he was getting chased by the cops. He was supposed to serve ten years, but I guess they reduced his sentence." Starving and finished with his story, Brad unwrapped a sandwich and began to eat.

Reluctant to admit she could see a long-term commitment with a butcher but dying to know more about his past, Julia asked about Tracey. "What took him to Atlanta? You've told me about your time in college, but I guess we haven't talked much about our families. Did Tracey go to school out there?"

Not sure how deep Brad wanted to get into his embarrassing family saga, he hesitated with a sip of beer. "Let's get more comfortable; this may take a while." An oversized two-person lawn chair had been permanently positioned on the platform at the end of the dock. Brad picked up two large cushions and nodded to the cooler before he led Julia over the water. Once they settled, he decided it was best to let it all out, he answered more than just her question.

"You see, it began many years ago. Like I said, my parents were married for thirty years before my mom finally found the courage to leave my dad. For as long as I can remember, he would spend all his free time at the Casinos—Choctaw in Durant until the WinStar opened in Thackerville. He was always chasing the next dollar. He won big a couple times, I mean big." Brad nodded. "But in the end, he lost everything."

"Oh no." Julia adjusted in the seat to get a better view of Brad's expression as he told the story. "How was he able to keep his land?"

Pausing to study Julia's face, Brad was unable to stop himself as he leaned in for a quick passionate kiss.

Julia didn't have enough time to close her eyes, yet the kiss took her breath away. She smiled and exhaled. "Wow."

"Sorry." A smile spread across Brad's face and his eyes twinkled. "Don't know what got into me. You're just so..." Then he kissed her again. This time, he removed his hat and allowed himself to pull her closer and enjoy the taste of her cherry Chapstick. He took his time and let his lips explore her jaw down to her neck while his hands roamed from the back of her neck, down her bare back, and ended on her thigh.

The sensation of Brad's hands on Julia's body and his lips on her neck left her skin tingling. Unable to get enough, she moved even closer and cupped his cheek with one hand before reaching behind his head to run her fingers through his hair. She almost forgot that they had been discussing his family until he backed away.

"Now it's my turn to say wow." As Brad caught his breath, he leaned his forehead against hers. "You drive me crazy, Julia." His husky tone made Julia's heart jump.

Captivated by Brad's brown eyes, she smiled before she leaned forward for one more kiss. "Where were we?" She repositioned herself far enough from him that they should be able to keep their hands off each other. "Your dad lost everything."

"Yeah, I was able to talk the bank into selling me his land for the repo price; I had no idea it was in jeopardy until about a week before it foreclosed. That's when my mom moved to Atlanta to be near her sister. Tracey moved out there the following year when he couldn't decide what to do to make a living. Apparently, stealing cars and selling drugs didn't work out so well for him. Neither of my brothers know the land is in my name now."

"Oh." Julia frowned. "So, your dad makes it up to you by working at the store." She nodded. "Makes sense." With an empathetic hand on his thigh, she said, "That's quite a family story, Brad."

"Can I be completely honest with you?" Brad asked.

"I wouldn't want you to be anything but."

"It took me a while to admit this to myself, but my parent's breakup is the reason I've never let anyone get close. I'm worried that I might do something to make my wife want to leave. I witnessed so much arguing and anger between my parents that I don't ever want to put someone I love through that kind of pain."

"Brad." Julia touched his cheek and sighed. "Thank you for sharing that with me. I understand. I don't remember a day that my parents didn't argue. If my dad wasn't drunk, he was sleeping. My mom pestered him about everything from not having a job to the way he tied his shoes, I swear."

When Julia paused, Brad nodded—his way of asking her to continue. She sighed. "You would think she'd figure out where his breaking point was, but she always pushed one step too far. Then she cried and expected everyone to feel sorry for her when she walked around with sunglasses on to hide the bruises." Julia huffed and shook her head. "If it were me and I had nowhere else to go and no one to run to for help, I would have at least stopped bitching before he hit me." *Which I learned all too early*, Julia thought.

"Honestly, my parents relationship taught me that any man I'm in a relationship with has to prove himself to me before I let myself fall—unfortunately a little too much." Her tone softened. "I'm really sorry that I didn't believe you. Jen and I have been friends forever and I trust her." Julia reached for Brad's hand, focused on his dark eyes, and continued. "Thank you for proving yourself to me. Now I can let myself fall." Her shy grin spoke volumes.

"You're everything I've been searching for, Julia. You are the most beautiful woman I've ever laid my eyes on," Brad admitted as he tucked a stray curl behind her ear and leaned closer. It seemed like a lifetime for Brad's lips to reach hers. "And my lips," he whispered then kissed her again. "And my hands." A mutual smile parted their lips and Julia welcomed his touch. When he paused, he confessed, "I've already fallen."

It was as if the warmth of the sun on her skin and the heat radiating from the man beside her were all that mattered; all her inhibitions disappeared. "It sure is hot today." Julia's voice deep with hunger left Brad wondering why she backed away. Until she smiled and stood, reaching for his hand. "Wanna go for a swim?"

Brad followed her lead and when Julia took a step toward the edge of the dock and lifted her tank top over her head, he gasped. Then she slid her skirt to the ground. Motivated by the vision of Julia's bare skin, Brad undressed faster than he ever had. By the time his clothes laid next to hers, Julia was halfway to the middle of the lake.

Once he caught up with her, he grabbed her around the waist and pulled her to him. Julia laughed loud enough for the sound to bounce across the water and off the trees. Brad covered her mouth with his and allowed their passion to take over. He reached under her thighs and lifted her into position.

Furrever Families

Saturday, July 18, 2020

"I HAD NO IDEA THIS place was even here." Julia turned to Brad as they sat inside his truck. A big red barn stood at the dead end of a private road with forty or more cars in the gravel parking lot. "How could I not know that an animal shelter was just ten minutes from my clinic?"

"Well, it is pretty new. The wife of one of my customers started this non-profit with four of her friends at the beginning of the year. This is the first adoption event they've had. Sherri tried to talk me into finding for a dog here before Charlie." Brad paused as he searched for the right phrase. "Found me? I guess." As he opened the door, he shook his head. That phrase didn't quite fit.

Before Julia had time to pull the lever on the passenger door, Brad had opened it and offered his hand. She tilted her head, "Chivalry isn't dead." A kiss on his cheek told him she appreciated his attention. They instinctively joined hands and headed to the entrance; laughter and a voice over the loudspeaker welcomed them as they walked through the door.

To the left was a substantial area with large enclosures that housed different breeds of dogs. To the right was another area with smaller enclosures that held cats of every shape and color. Multiple rooms had been sectioned off for the animals to meet and interact with their potential forever family. Each of the areas were closed off from the main part of the barn to control the level of noise. People, young and old, squatted down or sat in chairs as they cooed at and cuddled with the animals.

Julia's heart filled with gratitude; she had no idea there were so many people searching for a pet to complete their lives and silently thanked this organization for their hard work. "Wow, Brad. I'm in awe. I have to meet your friend's wife. I want to offer my services in some way; I want to be a part of this." Touched by the community coming together to support a cause to help homeless animals, Julia couldn't stop the stray tear as it rolled down her cheek. She tried to wipe it away before Brad noticed.

She realized she was too late, though, when he pulled her into a brief embrace and whispered in her ear,

"This is why I brought you here." Then he kissed her cheek. He released her, still holding her hand as he stared into her eyes. "This is why I can't stay away from you. You have the biggest heart."

"Brad, right?" A thin lady dressed in black slacks and a white button-up shirt approached. "I'm Kacy Schellenberger, President and co-founder of Furrever Families." She introduced herself and shook both of their hands. "Thanks so much for coming tonight. Our mutual friends matched your donation and I wanted to personally thank you. You have no idea how much that amount of money will help all the critters.

"We'll be serving a fantastic buffet meal in about twenty minutes. Please feel free to look around and mingle—oh, and don't forget to bid on some of our incredible silent auction items. I'll make it a point to catch up with you after things die down a bit." Kacy nodded to Julia. "A pleasure to meet you."

"Wow, a nice donation, huh?" Tilting her head, Julia offered a grin to the generous man beside her. "I'm impressed."

Through a set of double doors, long tables with white tablecloths lined three walls of the banquet area. Baskets of goodies, framed certificates, sports memorabilia, electronics, and small appliances were just a few of the items that had been positioned with silent auction bidding forms beside them. Professionally framed photographs of dogs and cats hung on the walls.

There must be a hundred people here, Julia thought as she noted the elegant ambiance of the event. Round tables with plants as centerpieces and crystal water glasses at each place setting had been strategically placed throughout the room. Many of the attendees were dressed in their Sunday best; Julia applauded herself for choosing to wear a simple sundress and sandals instead of shorts and flip-flops. Being underdressed surely would have left her feeling out of place and uncomfortable.

After they scrutinized the auction items and bid on their favorites, Brad led Julia to one of the round tables. She hung her purse on the back of her chair, turned to Brad, and smiled. "Kacy was right. There are a lot of great auction items to bid on. Did you see the Cowboys box-seat tickets? And how about the cruise from Galveston to Cozumel?" After an unexpected sigh, Julia closed her eyes and daydreamed of leaving her everyday life behind to soak up the warm sun as it shined on her face. "How wonderful would it be to get away for four nights?"

Unable to stay more than twelve inches from Julia, Brad made sure his chair sat close enough to rest his arm on the back of hers. He caressed her bare shoulder and focused on her voice.

"Nothing to do but lay beside the pool and sip on pina coladas all day. No barking dogs, no kitty litter to clean, no clients to console..." Julia's voice trailed off. When she opened her eyes, and noticed that Brad had been staring, she blushed, "I hear they have all kinds of entertainment, plays and magic shows. Some of the ships even have their own water park and casino's." With furrowed brows, she asked, "think we could ever get work off our minds?"

Brad chuckled and kissed her nose. "Doubtful. Although a few days away on a cruise with you does sound wonderful." The memory of swimming in the lake the night before brought heat to Brad's face. He leaned close to Julia. "Although, I think bathing suits are required on cruise ships."

"Not all of them." She lifted an eyebrow, then laughed as Brad's mouth dropped open. "I'm kidding, I'm kidding." Forcing her mind off their sexy swim, she turned the conversation back to the event. "Some smaller items are really nice, too. The wine and chocolate pairing basket from Marker Cellars Winery and the book basket filled with a romance series from a local author."

"Agreed. I saw you bid on the photography package—you have a session in mind?"

Julia lifted her shoulder in a half-shrug, "I donate

senior picture and family photo packages to a few families in need every year. A little way for me to give back. Some of my clients barely have the money to pay for groceries, but they find a way to care for their furry family members. I love that." Brad's intense scrutiny made her shiver and focus on her fingernails, "It's just a little something special for them."

"You just keep amazing me, Julia." The gentle tone of Brad's voice made Julia meet his gaze. "Every time we're together, I find another reason to want to spend more time with you." The pull to kiss her was almost impossible to resist. Brad cleared his throat and examined the crowd, finding an excuse to change the subject. "There must be a hundred people here."

Julia laughed. "You read my mind. Literally."

ᑎ ᑎ ᑎ

CHARLIE BOUNDED OUT the back door, putting weight on his broken leg every-other step. "I think the wild critters are making fun of him." Brad shook his head. "Poor dude has half a shaved ass."

An unanticipated laugh escaped Julia and she covered her mouth. For some reason, the statement caught her funny bone and she continued to chuckle as she watched the fluffy, white dog with one shaved hip and leg sniff around the fence. "Great Pyrenees are the best protectors, but they need so much room." Glancing at Brad, Julia added, "As you know. This property will be the perfect fit for Charlie once he's healed. I love that you have a fenced yard; it must help to know he's safe and won't get too far away until he's ready."

Brad grinned at the revelation that this beautiful woman sat beside him on his back porch, talking about everything and nothing. He thought he must be dreaming or that it had been too good to be true. He couldn't remember the last time he dated someone where there was no uncomfortable void to fill. It must have been years ago. He excused himself as he stood and returned with two glasses of wine.

"Thanks for stopping at my place so I could check on everyone." Julia accepted the glass.

"Whatever you need, sweetheart."

"I really need to find someone I trust to work an evening slash weekend shift, so I can do more things like this. Not only did I have a great time with you, but I also met some fantastic people. Networking is hard when you don't have much time to break away."

Flames from the fire in the pit provided the perfect amount of warmth to ward off the beginning of a chill in the night air. Brad sat beside Julia, leaned back, and put his arm behind her on the back of the chair. Heat radiated off her shoulders and Brad found himself caressing her flawless skin with his fingertips.

"You know, I used to dream about starting a shelter of sorts for smaller pets—something along the lines of Furrever Families. I told you a little about my first best friend, Hunter. He was the Great Pyrenees that I had when I was a kid."

Julia turned to face Brad and nodded. "I would love to hear more about him."

"We did everything together. Every morning when I went to do my chores, he waited for me in the same spot—just outside the door. He followed me to the bus stop and, for the longest time, I thought he waited there for me the entire day until I got home." A chuckle brought a twinkle to his eye.

"Stupid kid, huh? My brothers thought he was just a mangy pest and threatened to take him somewhere and drop him off when I didn't do what they wanted me to. Ridiculous things like do their barn chores, or chop firewood, or feed the chickens. I was so scared that one day they would take Hunter from me, so I did whatever they wanted. Until I got bigger.

"Once, when they made the threat, I called them out on it. I don't even remember what they wanted me to do, but when I didn't follow their demands and they started calling for Hunter, I punched Greg square in the jaw.

Dropped him. Surprised the shit out of both of us. We never told my dad because fighting was against the rules. Neither one of them ever said another word about Hunter."

"I love that." Julia's hand rested on Brad's thigh as he continued.

The smile faded, "One morning, he wasn't waiting for me when I went to do my chores. I called for him on the way out to the barn and thought he must have found a girl dog or something. You know how twelve-year-old boys think." He managed to grin.

"My stomach began to twist the longer Hunter didn't come when I called. I was almost ready to go back inside for breakfast, just needed to clean one last stall. When I called his name and really listened, I heard a whimper. My best guess is that he had been run over by a truck. It's the only thing that makes sense; a car wouldn't have done that much damage."

Julia gasped and covered her mouth with both hands.

"He was in a stall laying in dirty hay; his head and shoulder were covered with blood and he could barely make a sound. I knelt beside him and he tried to move, but growled. I knew he was in pain. I knew I had to help him, so I ran for my dad.

"You haven't met my dad yet, but let me assure you,

old age made him soft. Softer, anyways. Back then, to him, animals didn't have feelings and if you lived on a farm, you didn't call the vet. You took care of everything yourself. Because Hunter was mine, I had to do it."

In the distance, frogs and crickets called, but the sounds of nature couldn't soothe Brad's mind. "It took years for the nightmares to stop. I wasn't even thirteen when I was forced to kill my best friend."

"Brad..." Julia whispered and reached for his hand. "That's awful. I'm so sorry." Tears streamed down her cheeks at the thought of that poor little boy becoming a true rancher, according to his father's beliefs, before he was ready.

"I know what you think about my work, Julia." With tears in his eyes, Brad pursed his lips and looked deep into her eyes. "But I love animals. I have the utmost respect for nature and life, but I have to close off my emotions because I'm the one pulling the trigger."

Confused, Julia's heart moved quickly in the direction of falling for Brad, while her head moved the opposite direction. She remained unsure if she could fully, completely, and unconditionally love someone who killed animals for a living.

Instead of speaking, she touched his cheek, smiled, and blinked away her own tears; he closed his eyes and leaned into the palm of her hand. The compassionate man that sat beside her had been more open than any other man in her life. There was no way she would diminish what he confessed to her.

"I'm so glad you're here," he studied her expression. "I'm so pleased you had a good time tonight and I'm finding it hard to make myself stop thinking about you. Each time you enter my thoughts, I have to remind myself that I'm in the middle of a project, or driving, or talking to someone else. I literally have to focus to push you away." Brad placed his hand over hers and kissed her palm. "I'm falling for you, Julia. You've found a way to be everywhere."

Admitting the attraction to herself was one thing, but when she spoke the words out loud, she surprised herself. "You're not alone, Brad. Half of the day, I can't concentrate and the other half I struggle to focus. The way you look at me, the way you touch me, never leaves my mind. You're always there." Julia chuckled. "Hell, Jennifer even said I looked like I was walking on air. I can't remember the last time I've been this happy."

"You know if it wasn't for this dog, you and I would have never met." Brad smiled after Charlie finally settled beside his chair. The fur, soft against his palm, reminded him that there was nothing like having a four-legged best friend.

"If memory serves," Julia teased, "I believe you and

I were in a wedding together the following day. If it weren't for our friends, Lanie and Max, we may not have ever met." She paused to gauge his reaction. When Brad lifted one eyebrow, she continued. "The fact that you ran over a dog and dumped him at my clinic at four in the morning just means that I met the asshole side of you before I met the true loving, passionate, generous side of you."

"Ouch, I think?" Brad grimaced, put his hand over his heart, and played like he was confused by the statement.

"Yeah, like I could hurt your feelings. Whatever," Julia rolled her eyes and giggled. When she glanced back at Brad, her breath caught.

"My God, you're gorgeous," Brad's hungry eyes turned dark as he leaned toward Julia, silently suggesting she meet him halfway. She bit her bottom lip and tilted her head. When their lips touched, Brad sighed and slid closer. With one hand, he reached for Julia's hip and pulled her toward him.

She wrapped her arms around his neck and deepened the kiss. Unwilling to break away from the intense desire rising in her chest, Julia held her breath. She didn't want this feeling to end. Ever.

∩∩∩

"YOU KNOW WHAT I really want? What I've never had the gall to admit to anyone?" Julia pulled the sheet over herself as she turned on her side and rested her head on the pillow. She searched Brad's eyes for a sign that he wanted to hear more. He smiled and kissed her before she continued. "I want a man that sees me. Me. In the morning, with my hair all a mess and no makeup, stupid without coffee, and still think I'm beautiful. Not a twenty-nine-year-old woman, not a blonde, not a doctor. I want someone to see my soul. He needs to know how much I love my career, my friends, family, and my critters, of course."

"Twenty-nine," Brad's teasing tone did not go unnoticed. "Someone has a birthday coming up. A big one."

"Yeah," Julia sighed. "Good thing Lanie and Max already went back to Tennessee—she threatened to have a party for me. At least I don't have to worry about that."

"Mmm hmm." A rogue blonde curl fell over Julia's cheek and Brad couldn't resist reaching out to tuck it behind her ear. "You want to know what I see? Confidence. First and foremost, you know your shit and you're not afraid to show it. The first day we met, I was amazed at how attracted I was to someone that had just been shoved out of bed and into an emergency. For days, I told myself that it was just the situation, but quickly realized that it was so much more.

"Your passion continues to intrigue me. Your love for animals and your friends is beyond anything I've ever seen. I absolutely love that look you get when you're trying to prove your point. You hate to be wrong, don't you?" Brad inched closer while he pulled Julia to him. "And this. The way our bodies fit together?" After a gentle kiss, he smirked. "Perfection." He parted her lips and covered her body with his. "I love everything about you."

Surprise!

Friday, July 24, 2020

"I HAVE IT HERE somewhere," An older lady with hair so white it was almost blue dug through her purse in search of exact change.

"It's fine, you're good, Miss Pearl. Twenty cents won't break me." *My lord, this woman moves as slow as a sloth, not that I've ever treated a sloth so I wouldn't know, but still.* Julia kept a well-deserved sigh from escaping.

"Now, dear," she peered over reading glasses, voice shaky. "I don't like owing anyone anything. If you'll just give me another minute." As soon as she lifted her purse and prepared to dump out the contents, Julia stopped her and pushed the receipt into her hand.

"All set. You don't owe me a dime"—she chuckled and walked around the counter to lead the last client of the day to the exit door—"or even two. Have a nice day,

Miss Pearl."

All the end-of-day chores had been completed early so Julia could close on time. She had anticipated her date with Brad for days, an early dinner at a new barbecue joint in Bridgeport. He had spent the week in Denver at an annual meat conference. Before he left, he told her it was the best way to keep up with the latest technology, take some refresher courses, and network with others in the industry.

Even though they had talked on the phone a few times, it just wasn't the same as the sensation of his hand in hers or being able to steal kisses whenever she needed his touch. He had mentioned that he had something for her when he returned but refused to elaborate.

Julia loved surprises and looked forward to receiving something Denver-ish, but she let her mind wander to more romantic gifts. Maybe some massage oil or a sexy prompt card game; she wasn't quite ready for specialty couples engraving. *A couples cooking class may be fun.*

Thirty minutes later, the doorbell chimed and Julia's pulse quickened. She smiled at herself in the mirror and allowed a little squeal to escape. "Sucker." Unable to believe someone excited her this much so soon after meeting, she rolled her eyes at her reflection and hurried to the door.

Before she had a chance to speak, Brad wrapped her in his arms and pressed his lips to hers. The kiss quickly intensified and he backed her into the waiting room, closing the door behind them. Once they parted, both struggled to catch their breath. Brad stared into her eyes and grinned, "boy are you a sight for sore eyes." He framed her face with his hands, tilted her head to the exact position for maximum enjoyment, and kissed her again. "I can't believe how much I've missed your face."

Julia tightened her hold around Brad's shoulders and whispered, "me, too" against his lips. His muscles flexed under her touch. She didn't want to back away but felt the need to look at him, to examine his face for any signs of doubt. After all, her history with men proved that after a few weeks, the typical guy found a reason, any reason, to say it wasn't going to work. "Who would have guessed we would find each other after so much time searching? And giving up for me."

"Apparently your friend Lanie," Brad joked before turning serious. "You've brought so much enjoyment, passion, pleasure, to my life that I didn't even know I was missing. Not seeing you for a week was torture."

∩∩∩

"SURPRISE!" Startled, then stunned by ten voices that

called out in unison, Julia stopped mid-stride; her front foot inside the large dining room and behind her, a foot on tiptoe, ready to pivot.

The backroom of Raymond's BBQ had been decorated with birthday balloons, centerpieces on every table, and a black cat pinata in the corner. Several of Julia's closest friends, and a few regular clients, stood before her wearing party hats and genuine smiles.

As she examined each of her friends faces, joy and gratitude filled her heart. It was hard to grasp that all her favorite people would gather for her measly birthday celebration. Lanie and Max had flown in from Nashville, Pam and Jason had driven over an hour from Loving, and surely Teri and Jennifer had better things to do.

One face, though, drained the color from her cheeks and the joy from her soul. An aging man with shaggy gray hair, a dirty plaid, half-untucked shirt, and a sad smile stared at her. He stood far enough away from her friends to make it obvious that he was not one of them.

"What the fuck?" Julia whispered, unaware that anyone else in the room may have heard her.

A flashback from her childhood ran through her memory; her dad sat on a stump in the backyard and held a rabbit by the scruff. He made her watch him wring its neck to kill it, then skin it to prepare it for dinner. He talked the entire time about how he was the king of the house and all animals that roamed the planet were meant to feed the king and his family. The sounds that poor rabbit made still brought a chill to her arms.

"Sweetheart, are you ok?" Brad's arm wrapped around Julia's shoulder and he gave her a little squeeze. "You look upset."

"Why is he here?" Ignoring everyone else in the room, Julia focused on her father. The man she vowed to never speak to again. The man who had made her life a living hell for more years than she cared to remember. The same man that had driven her sister to a life filled with drugs and alcohol. Julia had done her best to hide her tumultuous home life from her friends after building a happy life in Texas. There was no reason, in her mind, to rehash the trauma of her teen years.

"I thought you would be excited to have some family here for your birthday," Brad's tone turned to a question. When they first walked in the door and Julia realized this was a party for her, she had smiled and raised her hands to her heart. Then Brad witnessed her reaction turn to anger to, what? Hurt? Disappointed? Disgust? in less than a second. Seemingly in slow motion, she turned to him with a scowl like he had never seen.

"What is wrong with you?" Julia hissed, then cleared her throat and shook her head. The last thing she wanted was to show weakness in front of her dad, but she failed. "How could you do this to me?" Tears streamed down her face as she gasped for air. Staring into the eyes of the man she loved, Julia spoke words she never imagined would be directed at Brad. "I don't want to see you again. Ever." Furious and shaking, she turned to leave.

∩∩∩

THE DOORBELL RANG for the tenth time, followed by knocking and Brad's muffled voice. Julia could make out some of the words—"I'm sorry" and "Julia, please talk to me"—but she covered her ears and moved to the furthest place in the house from the front door. Brad must have tired of pounding on the door because after about an hour, the noise stopped and she no longer heard his voice.

The last thing she wanted to do was explain why she continued to let her shitty childhood affect her adult life. Visions of her brothers and sisters huddled in a corner as their dad hit their mom and the smell of alcohol on his breath when he tried to kiss her had almost been erased from her mind. Until about a few hours ago. That horrible man should have been in prison for the things that he did to his own children.

One memory brought a little comfort; the one where Julia secretly wished her father to be in an accident, so he wouldn't be waiting for her when she came home from school. She envisioned his death almost every night from the time she was ten until she went to college.

When Julia found enough courage to tell her mom what had happened, she had told her daughter to quit telling lies. "If you lie now, no one will ever believe you when you tell the truth."

After Julia moved to Lansing for college, her little sister showed up in her dorm; she had run away from the man that had been sexually abusing her for three years. Thankful that she had only been physically abused, Julia convinced her sister to go to the police, but their mother refused to press charges.

From then on, Julia pretended that he went to prison, as he should have, and even wrote a letter to him stating that he was dead to her. She made a conscious choice to remember the very few good things from her childhood and forget that she even had a father.

She was thankful that Lanie drove her home from Bridgeport and that she did her best to try to calm Julia, to talk her off the ledge, but tears and hiccups prevented a real conversation. Julia didn't have it in her to explain her entire messed up youth, so she convinced Lanie that she would be fine and just wanted to go to bed. She promised her friend that they would talk it out later in the week.

∩∩∩

RED AND ORANGE streaked the sky as the sun set. Puzzled by the turn of events, Brad sat on Julia's steps and struggled to figure out what went wrong. *Don't we have something special? We're just getting started. I wanted Julia's birthday to be extra special, made arrangements with all her closest friends to help celebrate; Lanie and Max came from Nashville, for God's sakes. Obviously, I missed something about Julia's dad. When Sherri offered to help, I provided names and locations. Who knew she would find him in Fort Worth?*

The entire weekend had been planned for Julia's thirtieth birthday, complete with a concert at Brad's property. After the botched surprise dinner, Brad told the group he would meet them back at the stage area in a little while and to head over there without him. No sense in wasting a good party, even if the person they were celebrating didn't show.

A structure built with two-by-fours and plywood supported Brad and Max as they sat in plastic chairs. "Remember when we made this stage? We were so young. Who knew where life would take us? Man, we had some wild nights out here. Your dad never made much of a fuss, but he knew what we were up to, right?" Max leaned back and picked at the strings of his guitar.

Focused on the cowboy hat in his hands, Brad leaned forward with his forearms on his knees. "How could he not know with my brothers tattling on me about everything?" He grinned. "It was so peaceful after Greg went off to college and Tracey discovered girls. I couldn't wait for them to leave me alone and just let me do my thing."

Taillights from the last of the party guests disappeared on the trail. "Remember the last time we played here?" Max's voice lowered along with his spirit. "Ol' what's her name started a fight with Jerry because she watched him trying to get with some drunk girl behind the cabin. She should have known he was cheating on her months before that night. I mean, seriously, he was the bass player in a country band. That's what we did."

Brad shook his head and laughed. "You tried to break it up and Jerry fell off the stage. I still can't believe he thought you pushed him. Hell, he didn't even remember what happened the next day when he woke up in the hospital with a cast on his arm. A shame he believed everyone else over you. We never played together again. What a waste of talent."

Crickets filled the silence as Max thought of the right words to ask about what happened earlier in the night. He decided to just spit out the most direct question he could think of. "So, how's Julia?"

Brad sighed. "She didn't answer the door or the phone. I sat on her front steps until the concrete grew cold. I guess she must need the time alone. Right? I just wish she would talk to me. I don't know what happened, what went wrong. I mean, she told me that her dad was a jerk when she was a kid, but she never said that she hates him. Watching her reaction was about enough to kill me; I feel like the biggest tool in the shed.

"I need to make it up to her. I can't lose her, man. She's seriously the best thing that's ever happened to me. That sounds so stupid." He felt his friend staring at him, so he raised his eyes.

Max nodded and a knowing smile spread across his lips. "No. It really doesn't. I totally understand. I felt that with Lanie not so long ago. Listen," Max continued. "Lanie took her home. She'll get to the bottom of this. We'll get this fixed." He slapped Brad on the shoulder and asked, "Hey, have you sung any of your songs to Julia yet? Does she know what a great songwriter you are?"

Brad raised his eyebrows in question.

"You know, like the one you wrote for Ellie. It

didn't really mean anything to that selfish little girl, but the words fit perfectly for the way you feel about Julia. Don't they?"

Brad leaned back in his chair. "Man, I almost forgot about that song. How many years ago was that? Do you still think it means the same thing after all this time?"

"If it comes from your heart, it'll last forever. That's evergreen, man. If you feel the same emotions for Julia and your love is true, then that song will live on for years. As a matter of fact, I was going to ask if I could buy the rights from you."

Brad smiled. "Brother, it's yours." A handshake sealed the deal.

Home in Paradise

Saturday, July 25, 2020

A FADED PIECE OF lined paper, delicate from being folded and opened so many times, sat on the table in front of Brad. He read and re-read the words as he tried to conjure memories of his high school love.

She was a little pushy at the time and he could only imagine if he had stayed with her. They crossed paths last year in the local grocery store and she glared at him from the deli area. Her husband and four kids followed like the good little disciples she turned them all into. A shudder rolled through him; *glad I dodged that bullet.*

After scratching out a couple words and changing a few of the lyrics, Brad shook his head, crumpled the paper, and tossed it into the garbage can. Those words had been intended for someone else. He needed to create a song with better words; words with emotions he felt for Julia and Julia alone. *This has to be perfect.*

Brad leaned back in the chair, closed his eyes, and concentrated on his breathing. Visions of Julia danced in his head; his heart filled with love and a smile reached his lips. An hour later, after the words flowed from Brad's heart to the pad of paper in front of him, he beamed with pride and wished he knew how to play guitar. *It'd be too much of an inconvenience to ask Max to come with me, wouldn't it?*

∩∩∩

ALTHOUGH MARKER Cellars Winery had always been the girls' go-to place to meet. Lanie felt they needed a more neutral area where no one knew them. Julia locked the clinic doors and drove twenty miles south to The Sweet Taste of Paradise Winery so she and Lanie could talk in private.

Tables dotted the covered patio that overlooked the vineyard; Lanie and Julia strolled to a secluded area and made themselves comfortable. Lanie breezed right past small talk and asked how Julia was holding up.

"I had to push Brad to the side of my thoughts just long enough to make it through a few customers this morning. Teri, of course, can read me like a book, so she immediately knew something was wrong." The red in her eyes from the tears had cleared, but they were still a little puffy.

"So," Lanie began, "I may be an ass for saying this, but I can't let you throw this relationship away." Warm fingers covered Julia's hand offering comfort. "Y'all are so right for each other. So much better than I would have ever thought. I just can't accept the fact that you won't be together. This must be just a really unfortunate misunderstanding. You both deserve the truth. Full disclosure. Transparency." Lanie tilted her head and smiled. "I really think you need to talk this out."

Wine flowed into their glasses. One sip, then another, loosened Julia's nerve enough to be totally honest with her friend, once and for all. Still watching the legs run down inside of the glass, Julia said, "He sent flowers. They're just gorgeous; exactly what I love. I was going to throw them in the trash, but Teri talked me into keeping them. She said, 'Because sometimes we just need a little pretty'." Lifting her gaze, Julia confirmed the statement as fresh tears filled her eyes. "She's not wrong."

"Talk to me, Julia. Please. Let me help you."

"I'm just so mad because he didn't ask me before inviting him. It's really hard to talk about my childhood." Another sip of wine gave Julia courage. "You know I grew up pretty poor. My dad never worked, never provided for his family. He was an alcoholic, abusive to everyone, and didn't know how to show love. I doubt he's even capable."

Over the next hour, Julia explained how her dad would verbally belittle and physically abuse the entire family. He forced them to obey his ridiculous house rules, refused to buy any birthday or Christmas gifts, or even allow anyone to be taken to the hospital when they got sick.

"I had this friend in sixth grade. I asked my mom if I could go to her house for a sleepover and was stunned when she said yes. We were never allowed to go to anyone else's house. So, when I got there, my friends mom gasped when she saw me. Literally. I didn't think about it at the time, but years later, I figured out why.

"She took me directly to the kitchen, made some mac and cheese, and sat the bowl in front of me. I just looked at her in disbelief. We weren't allowed food like that, let alone more than one helping. After I ate the entire box, she led me to the bathroom and ran the shower for me. It wasn't Wednesday, my bath day, so I wasn't sure how to react. My dad would hit us if we wasted water." Julia finished and pursed her lips as she gazed into the pasture.

Tears rolled down Lanie's cheeks faster than she could wipe them away. She listened to details of a childhood that no one should ever have to endure, she envisioned a horror film. She held her friend's hand, "I'm so sorry, Julia. I didn't know. Brad invited your dad, so he must have thought y'all made up? Wait. Julia," Lanie sat forward to secure her friends full attention. "Did you tell Brad about all this? Does he know the entire story? Does Sherri?"

Julia shook her head and sighed. "No. I only told him that he was a jerk growing up."

"Then how would they possibly be able to know what a horrible idea this was? They both love you and wanted to do something so special for your big birthday."

Hope made Julia sit up straighter. "You think he loves me?"

Lanie raised her eyebrows and nodded.

A frown pushed the hope away. "Well, even if he does, I couldn't seriously spend the rest of my life and raise my kids with a man that processes animals for a living. It goes against everything I believe in."

Before Julia could say another word, Lanie laughed. "Girl, stop trying to talk yourself out of a good thing." She shook her head. "If what's in your heart is truly love, then you can't let this go. You'll regret it, I promise." Lanie squeezed Julia's hand and added, "It's always easier just to say goodbye and get over it but, trust me, that one true love is so worth the fight."

Julia sipped the wine and studied the grapes on the vines in the distance. She mulled over Lanie's words and confessed, "I guess I may have blown it out of proportion." A light breeze blew through Julia's hair and she took a minute to think about the consequences of not going after her man. She exhaled and found the support of her friend. "Did I blow it?"

"No. I don't think so. We'll fix this."

∩∩∩

UNABLE TO SLEEP, JULIA stared at the ceiling above her bed. Thoughts about what to say to Brad, how and when to say the exact right words made her restless. *Could he be the one? I haven't had these kinds of feelings for anyone. Ever. He's so perfect for me. He gets me, sees the real me.*

Music drifted through the open window along with a breeze that moved her sheer curtains. *Did I leave the radio on in the clinic? Oh, my God, what if someone broke in? Wait, why would anyone turn up the radio if they're breaking in somewhere that's really stupid. I must be delirious.*

Julia rolled out of bed and peeked out her bedroom window. *Just in case there is an intruder, I don't want to be seen.* She recognized Brad standing in her yard and gasped. *What the hell is he doing here?*

Julia heard a guitar strum, but Brad held only a single rose. She gazed around the yard and saw Brad's pickup backed up to her yard; Max and Lanie sat on the tailgate. Max held his guitar on his lap and played a beautiful melody.

Lanie had helped the men create an irresistible scene with what Julia thought must be a hundred lit candles spread throughout the yard. A string of white lights crisscrossed the yard and illuminated Brad from above. He stood with his head down, his black cowboy hat covered his face, one hand rested in his front pocket, the other held the rose.

When the first words flowed from Brad's lips into the air, Julia's knees went weak. The second he lifted his head, peered out from under the rim of his hat, and found her eyes, her heart connected to his. That was the moment she knew for sure.

> *Climb up in my Jeep; Let's take her*
> *for a ride*
> *I don't want to live another day*
> *without you by my side*
> *There's so much more I want to do*
> *with you*
> *Stay with me in Paradise*
> *When I'm with you I'm Home in*

Paradise

Home in Paradise

From the tailgate, Max whispered, "That's not the same song from high school."

Brad nodded. "Yeah I wrote a new one." He turned to face his friend and gave a sly smile.

Max lowered his head, shook it, and hid a smirk.

That day at the lake If birds could,

they would cover their eyes

I can still hear your laugh bounce off

the trees

There's so much more I want to do

with you

Stay with me in Paradise

When I'm with you, I'm Home in

Paradise

Home in Paradise

Hot days at the winery lead to even

hotter Texas Summer Nights

In the morning with your hair all a-

mess

You're more gorgeous than the night

before

There's so much more I want to do to

you

Stay with me in Paradise

When I'm with you I'm Home in
Paradise

Home in Paradise

I know you feel it, too I see how you
walk on air

Just let yourself fall; I promise I'll
catch you, I'll be right here

Take a chance; roll the dice

Let's build our own little Paradise

There's so much more I want to do
with you

Stay with me in Paradise

When I'm with you I'm Home in
Paradise

Home in Paradise

Thunder clapped in the distance and rain began to
fall. The candles flickered as the wind picked up, but
Brad didn't flinch. Lanie grabbed an umbrella from the
back of the truck and held it over Max as he played.

Come with me baby take my hand

Let's build a life on a little piece of
land

Raise a little family in our own
Paradise

Stay with me in Paradise

> *I can see it now*
> *Critters and kids running wild*
> *We will make it our own Paradise*
> *Let's make a home in Paradise*

When the music stopped, Brad removed his hat and Julia wiped the tears from her cheeks. As if reading the other's thoughts, they mouthed "I love you" in unison.

After the Rain

Sunday, July 26, 2020

SUNLIGHT SHONE through the curtains in Julia's bedroom. Birds chirped in the trees outside her window. Memories of the previous night brought a smile to Julia's lips, swollen from hours of kissing Brad after he serenaded her.

"Good morning, beautiful," Brad's voice, deep from sleep, reached Julia's ear.

She sighed and snuggled closer under his protective arm. Her arm wrapped around his waist as she tried to get closer, even though it was impossible. She knew they needed to have a serious conversation but dreaded ruining such a joyful mood.

"You want to get up, so we can talk, or just do it here?" Brad read her mind and gave her the option.

"Mmm. I don't want to move. How about here?"

Brad tightened his hold on her and kissed the top of

her head. "I'll start. I want to apologize again for inviting your dad without running it past you first. I'm so sorry that I upset you."

When Julia started to speak, Brad said, "I know, I apologized a hundred times last night, but I wanted to say it one final time."

She nodded into his chest and ran her fingers through the short hair before letting her hand roam.

"You have to stop touching me like that or I won't be able to finish."

She giggled. "Okay. Continue."

"I should have been more upfront and honest with you sooner. I knew that my work bothered you and, I don't know"—he shrugged under the weight of her head—"I guess I figured if we were a match, it would just work, it wouldn't matter. I was wrong and I'm sorry." He brushed his fingers along her cheek. .

"What I most want you to know is that none of the harvested animal is wasted. None of it goes unused. I support nonprofits and give to the less fortunate as much as I can."

"Really?" Julia raised herself to lean on her elbow so she could gauge his expression.

"Really. One day a week, I have a free ground beef day. Anyone in need within our community is welcome to stop by the store and get two pounds of beef."

"Brad..."

"My dad handles the physical part of that and turns in numbers to me each week. You'd be surprised at how many kids need more meals than their parents can afford to give them."

"I'm amazed. I don't know what to say. That's fantastic. I'm so proud of you. I need to be honest too. First, that just changed my entire perception of what you do, well some of it anyway. To put it bluntly, I'm trying to wrap my head around being in love with someone who kills animals."

Brad rolled his eyes and tried to move. Julia held him in place. "I told you I would be blunt. If you love me, you love all of me."

"You're right," he said and kissed her. "I'm sorry. Please continue."

"I meant it when I said I'm proud of you. When we first met, I couldn't see past the actions needed to do what you do. Now, I think if I turn it around into a positive and consider how much good you're doing for Paradise, I can get past it." It was her turn to kiss him and he smiled.

He pulled her to him and wrapped her in an embrace in which she never wanted to leave. Unfortunately, she needed to speak her peace too.

"Okay. Now it's my turn. I want to apologize again

for taking my anger out on you. I know you were trying to make my birthday special. I haven't told many people about my childhood, it's so embarrassing. But I promised myself I would tell you everything. I only pray that you will still love me."

Brad released her so she could get more comfortable and he rolled on his side. "I promise I will still love you."

"I'm sorry that I haven't been completely open about this, but I didn't know how much I cared for you, or rather, wouldn't let myself fall, until a few days ago. Honestly, I thought it could wait. Obviously, it can't."

"Spit it out, sweetheart."

"Okay. Here goes. The long and short of it is my mom was weak, my dad was a dick, us kids suffered. Seeing my dad again upset me for so many reasons. Not only because of the abuse when I was young, although that's the basis of the reason. When I was in college, I found out that my dad had abused my youngest sister. Had been for years" She glanced at Brad and closed her eyes to stop the tears before they fell. "Sexually. She's the only one. I don't know why. Maybe because she was the least verbal? The rest of us kids deserved our punishment most of the time." After a sigh, Julia said, "My mom refused to press charges against my dad."

"After years of battling with my family over it,

getting nowhere, I decided that it would be best for me, mentally, to pretend that he went to prison. Anyway, I wrote a letter to him stating that he was dead to me. I chose to never think about him again, moved to Texas, and started a veterinary business in a small town where no one knew me. I could be anyone I wanted; I decided to be the true me, the me that had been silenced for most of my young life.

"There's so much more that I haven't told you, so many instances of what I thought was a normal way for parents to treat their kids. When I got to college and had the freedom to go to my friends' houses for the weekend or just to escape for a night, I realized that the way my family lived was very dysfunctional. Dads should never tell their daughters that they're stupid and don't have enough brains in their head to get into college, let alone have a career.

"I didn't tell you everything before because it's so humiliating. The good that I choose to take from it is that it made me defiant and forced me to become the exact opposite of him. It's still not something that I like to admit or talk about. I've tried to bury it for so many years." Julia didn't anticipate so many emotions rising to the surface. The tears began to flow freely.

Brad pulled her into a hug and rocked her, letting her cry. "Shh. Baby, I'm here. I'm here."

When she was able to take a few deep breaths, Brad released her and told more of his experience from planning her party, "When Sherri got in touch with your mom, she and your siblings all refused the invitation; everyone had something else to do or couldn't get away on such short notice."

"Or so they said."

"Or so they said." He nodded. "She also gave Sherri your dad's information. Once she found him, he told her that he had been living in a halfway house for six months and could finally travel out of the DFW area. Great timing, huh? He sounded excited to catch up with his eldest daughter after so many years apart." Brad kissed the top of Julia's hair. "I'm so sorry, sweetheart. If I had known, I wouldn't have ever reached out to your family. I feel like such a shit."

"Don't apologize. Please. To be honest, I actually feel a lot better than I have in years. I haven't talked to anyone about this since, well, ever. Lanie forced me to talk, so she knows a few stories, but no one else," Julia lifted her head and smiled. She touched Brad's face; his whiskers tickled her palm. "I guess I should thank you for helping me overcome my past."

"Anything for you, my love," he half-teased and planted a quick kiss on her lips.

"I have to tell you that, last night, that song. Just

wow. Who sings that one? I've never heard it. How did you find something that sounds just like us? Gave me all the feels. You really know how to make a girl fall, don't you?"

He smiled and presed his lips against her nose. "I love you, too, Julia. I used to write songs for the band. Once we broke up, I stopped writing. Max used to say I was going to make a mint selling lyrics to some big producer; I just laughed him off."

"You? You wrote that? When? It's beautiful." She gasped and raised her hand to her heart. "For me? Oh, Brad," Julia wrapped her arms around his neck and kissed him in a way that allowed her to express how much she appreciated him. "I love you," she whispered against his lips.

"Whew. Damn, girl. You're going to get me going again." After he caught his breath, he answered her question. "Last night, when I was trying to figure out how to convince you to be mine, I let my heart guide my hand."

"You just keep surprising me, don't you? On top of having a huge..." Julia lifted one eyebrow as her hand travelled down his belly. "Heart," she laughed as Brad play-growled, "You're also pretty damn sexy; your voice is hypnotizing."

Brad rolled on his side, brushed the hair from Julia's

eyes, and started to sing.

Just let yourself fall; I promise I'll
catch you, I'll be right here

Kisses rained down on her.

Come with me baby take my hand

The whispered lyrics in her ear made her shiver with anticipation.

Let's build a life on a little piece of
land

She groaned and wrapped her hands in his hair as his lips trailed down her neck.

Raise a little family in our own
Paradise

He hummed the song as he kissed his way down to her chest and back to her lips.

Julia smiled and gripped his hips as he positioned himself above her.

Stay with me in Paradise

Epilogue

Saturday, July 31, 2021

THE BEAT OF THE BASS guitar and drums matched Julia's heartbeat. It had always been on her bucket list to travel to Nashville and enjoy the live music along Broadway. The fact that she had been lucky enough to spend her honeymoon here with the man of her dreams made it the best vacation ever.

She and Brad barely slept the previous night, after they said their "I do's" in front of their closest friends and family. The time spent with Lanie and Max had been exhilarating enough to keep them energized. Who knew being a country music star could be so fantastic?

"The next little ditty we're going to play was written by one of my best friends and a fantastic song writer," Max pointed off-stage to Brad. "This one's called Paradise. I hope y'all like it."

Brad wrapped his arm around Julia's shoulder and

she raised her hand to entwine their fingers. The diamond ring, a heavy, gorgeous reminder that she and Brad had just gotten married, reflected the stage lights.

From the side of the stage, Lanie grinned at her friends with pride.

∩∩∩

"WHEN IT BEGAN TO rain, y'all just pushed through. I didn't even notice until the candles went out, then I glanced at Lanie and she was holding an umbrella over Max. Seriously, all y'all are so sweet. Truly, the best day of my life." Julia's smile hadn't faltered in the last two days. "Well, until yesterday, that is. And last night, just...wow." She closed her eyes and inhaled. Her friends giggled beside her.

Lanie, Julia, and Pam sat on one side of the table and reminisced about the previous year as they nursed glasses of white wine. The boys talked business over whiskey.

"Brad, I have a proposition for you." Max lifted his glass for another sip.

As he leaned back in the leather lounge chair, Brad lifted his chin. "I'm listening."

"What would you say if I asked you to write songs for the band? You know, like the good ol' days?" Before

Brad had a chance to speak, Max raised his hand, palm out, and shook his head. "Wait, let me finish. I've already talked to my producer and he's going to make you an offer for the rights to that song you wrote in high school and 'Paradise'. You're one of the best and I want to work with you on a regular basis. What do you say?"

The amber liquid swirled in the glass and Brad admired the color as he chuckled. "Yeah, ok. Good joke, old friend." When Max didn't laugh in response, Brad raised his head to find his friend staring at him. "You're serious?"

"As a heart attack." Max nodded. "We have a meeting in the morning. I want you to be there."

"Max. I'd be honored."

Thank you for reading!

Please consider writing a short review wherever you purchased, rented, or borrowed this book. Reviews help readers find their new favorite stories and authors improve their craft.

Also by Kristi Copeland

TEXAS SUMMER NIGHTS

OTHER WORKS

About the Author

KRISTI COPELAND is the author of contemporary and book club fiction. She lives in Texas with her husband and multiple critters on their ranch. When she's not writing, Kristi enjoys spending time with close friends, wine tasting, and cat collecting.

www.kristicopelandwriter.com

Let's get social :

Kristi Copeland (Instagram)

Kristi Copeland - Writer (Facebook)

Kristi Copeland (Goodreads)

Made in the USA
Columbia, SC
12 June 2022